Affie Blake was born in Cork and lives in Dublin but has lived in, amongst other places, Oxford, Paris, and Hastings. Having worked as an educator for twenty-five years, Affie has also written three novels and a volume of poetry – *Learn by Mosaic* is the first to be published.

Published by Piwaiwaka Press
Copyright © Affie Blake 2024

Cover artwork: Mairéad Hannon
Cover design: Madden Hay

Learn by Mosaic

Affie Blake

Piwaiwaka
Press

For Helen Wheeler

One

'I don't think I scream damaged goods, do I?' Lil inhaled scanning Keith's face for a response.

He was lighting another cigarette and looked inquiringly at her.

Lil continued.

'I would just love to know what it's like, to be emotionally and mentally stable, what that must feel like, even for just an afternoon. Very serene I'd imagine.'

Keith exhaled.

'No you wouldn't,' he said, shaking his head. 'Very boring,' he matter-of-facted. 'All that zen.'

'I want all that zen!' shrieked Lil. 'It must be so nice, wafting around all zenned out. I should try weed,' she paused. 'Actually no, I shouldn't.'

She inhaled again looking at Keith willing him to say something to soothe everything.

He was looking into the distance.

'Keith,' she began, 'You're pretty stable, really, I think.'

He shrugged. 'That's what you think,' he laughed faux demoniacally.

Lil paid no heed to this.

'You are. You have a stable relationship, stable family – ish – and you even have stable eating habits. What you eat looks pretty hideous, but you still eat properly.' She looked away. 'Porridge for lunch,' she said more to herself, and shuddered. 'Porridge anytime.'

She lit another cigarette. She could feel the adrenaline start to surge through her body. It practically had a pulse. She was agitated. She flicked her cigarette.

'We have got to get this down, it needs to be right,' she said. 'We need to be right, professional, and convincing.'

She stood up straight to emphasis her point.

'Don't worry about it,' said Keith. 'It'll be fine.'

Lil was displeased.

'We don't know that it'll be fine – it could be very far from fine. I'm sure Chicken Curry's not fine. I'll bet he's far from fine. He's probably furious, and we can't really blame him.'

Lil sighed, panic was beginning to rise, and she urgently wished Keith would display some sense of understanding and commitment to the gravity of their situation.

He didn't.

'Stop worrying, he'll be fine. If he asks us, which he probably won't, we'll explain and it'll be fine. Relax, have another cigarette.'

He extended one.

She took it, lit it, exhaled.

'We can't wait for him to find us, we need to go to him, we have to be seen to care, we need to tell him, get in first, it's more respectful.'

Keith exhaled.

'You're overreacting,' he said.

Lil inhaled again to hide her exasperation.

'I am not – this is the proper, professional way. Now, let's go over it again, so we have our story straight, and we don't mess it up.'

Lil and Keith stood, stinking of tobacco and with the vapour of stale lager dampening the air around them, in front of he-who-shall-not-be-curried-with, Chicken Curry, in his office. Lil was sweating with shame. Her whole body was prickly and hot from humiliation and lack of water – twenty million cups of coffee that morning had done nothing to rehydrate her crazed mind or jittering body. She felt twitchy and itchy and not nice, oh dear. She could feel her eyebrows collapsing in on themselves, not a good look she thought grimly, for a thirty something singleton. Yesterday's clothes too, she also thought without needing to look down.

Chicken Curry stood tall and gazed down his long Roman nose at them. A nose that was long and straight like a middle finger, bent at the knuckle, just before it raps on a window of a house containing two genteel spinster sisters of old; rapping on the pane as the two look up from their needlework to see gleaming teeth at the window laughing in at them, causing them to hither and thither up to bed, reminded not only that they too shall die one day, but that on the whole people are bastards.

'I shall not be curried with,' said Chicken Curry, looking down on them. 'Could you tell me exactly what happened?'

He stared enquiringly at Lil.

Her eyes widened as, panic-stricken, she cleared her throat – suddenly very, very dry – and brushed her sleeve. She needed a glass of water. And had an image of how she must look, some buxom slatternly wench from mock Tudor times, with blotchy skin, blurry vision, and a filming over her teeth. God. French people had told her looked special, which she had taken as a compliment to her general look. A look which reflected her bank balance not her personality. She discovered quite by chance the true meaning, which was more 'special' as in a 'has your carer just popped out for a second, pet?' rather than 'you look amazing come here and kiss me.'

She sighed.

Bloody French. They're so bourgeois, bored, and blasé all the time. As soon as they're born, the babies probably look around at the new world and then slap the doctor. What would the bloody French know, anyway?

She gulped and looked at Chicken Curry.

He was waiting.

Lil clicked into gear. But Keith jumped in. Thank god, thought Lil as Chicken Curry's eyes flicked from her. She could still feel the burn of his incredulity. She wasn't sure if she wished she was dead or not. No, not dead, just younger, more gorgeous, not working here, and with a fabulous wardrobe. She realised if she had been alive in Tudor, mock or not, times, she was now so old that she would've been dead. And now. She was confused. This is not good, she thought.

Keith seemed unperplexed.

Chicken Curry nodded and looked at her again. Horror flashed through her as she realised that she had missed whatever had just been said. Keith was smiling and shrugging his shoulders in that self-effacing nonchalant way of his. Lil sort of smiled, falsely, having no real idea of what was going on. Her brain was fogged over.

'I suppose we can leave it at that, I imagine it won't happen again,' said Chicken Curry.

With a touch of sternness, noted Lil.

'Never,' she effused.

Chicken Curry looked her over, she could feel his gaze, and blushed. He thinks I'm insane, she thought. I am becoming that person, the one who's useless but understood to be an accredited lateral thinker, and quirky, now discovered to be in fact just useless. And old. Too old. Dear god.

Lil and Keith thanked him for his time, left, and headed straight outside for a cigarette.

'That went well,' said Keith.

Lil was not remotely convinced.

'He thinks I'm a complete idiot,' she moaned. 'Out of my mind. I really should know better, Keith. I am older than you.' She sighed, 'And he's right, what in the hell were we thinking?'

Keith was beginning to flag.

'It wasn't the worst,' he said. 'I've slept here before.'

Lil looked upward, 'Yes, but the bloody police didn't come then! Goddamn that alarm.'

She sighed again.

Keith laughed.

Then she laughed, too.

'We shouldn't laugh,' she said. 'How the hell did they know my name?'

They both laughed again.

'Yikes,' she said, 'I don't have the energy to wonder how. Probably saw my photo at reception.' She lit another. 'We can't tell anyone about this. Everyone thinks we left when the police left, so if anyone asks – '

Keith nodded, he was getting tired now.

'At least he bought the *I left my car keys here* line. My car's at home. Hope he hasn't noticed that.'

Lil, too, was getting tired and finding it harder to care.

'Did we get rid of the bottles?' she asked.

'Yes, remember?' he answered.

She nodded.

'Thank goodness for that. I've two more classes. Students were looking at me like I'd had a domestic situation. Never again.'

They smiled at each other.
'Until the next time,' laughed Keith.
'Never!' said Lil.

Later, the sun was of course beaming brightly, shining, and heating the air. Trees were swaying, birds were singing, and people were smiling. Laugher tinkled through the ether, and some mild mood minded folk were having ice creams. Poets wrote of days such, which made the blind see, the cynics believe and love's lambent loveliness clear and generous for all.

Not for Lil.

She was stumbling home, with her fingers and face clenched as she sweated and swore to herself under her overcoat, which being too heavy to carry she had put on, in a rage of the injustice of life and money. She blinked away flashbacks of *going just for just one, or three,* and going back to work at two a.m., setting off the alarm, running away, coming back, abashed, meeting the police like badly behaved school kids, and then trying to sleep on high backed office chairs.

Never again she gritted.

I need a drink, she thought and slunk into the first bar she passed.

The shade after the glare outside pleased her – it was a relief, a refuge. She walked up to the bar. The sole barman was cleaning a glass. He didn't notice her, or chose not to, she thought. He was polishing the glass like it was the crown jewels! It's one bloody glass. She took out her wallet hoping the jingle of cash would get his attention. Gathering herself before speaking, hoping to look composed, dignified, regal even, she saw herself in the mirror behind the bar. She looked decomposed, undignified, and common. As muck, she thought. Even my face is grubby, or maybe that's the beginning of a tan? I hate tans. Most likely the smuts from another day of thankless chore. The remnants she thought, I'm a bloody remnant, the dinosaur in the midst.

She looked at the barman again.

He was still rubbing.

And met her eye.

She started, as though she had been rumbled peeking through a chink in the curtain in the boys' changing room, everyone knowing she had been there wishing to see them in their underclothes.

God she thought.

'Are you alright?' he asked.

Lil fluffed a bit until she realised he was asking her what she wished to order, and mentally reminded herself that she really needed to learn how to speak normally. It can't be that difficult, everyone does it. Generally. She stopped, thinking, remembering she was on the verge of being a crazy woman.

'Two glasses of red,' she chirped. 'Thank you.'

She smiled. Damn you, you judgemental bastard, she thought.

'What would you like?' he asked.

Lil flushed with embarrassment, 'Two glasses of red,' she repeated confused.

'Do you have a preference?' he asked.

'Just wet,' she laughed with an *I'm so casual and cool and an uncaring sort of girl* laugh. Dying inside. Crash course in the normal language, she thought and smiled and nodded again thanking him as she paid, leaving a generous *forgive me, I'm actually great and normal* tip and went away.

Outside in the smoking area she unburdened herself of her overcoat and sighed heavily as she sat down. She took a large swig from glass number one and lit a cigarette. She looked around. People were finishing work now, their normal jobs, going home, having dinner, talking about their day, having a glass of wine, talking to their kids, watching TV. All very normal, I probably wouldn't like it anyway, she thought, I'm sure they would get on my nerves, all that day-to-dayer humdrum dreg and drag.

She took another swig and gazed into the distance. It must be nice, though, to feel vaguely satisfied in an *it's not perfect but I wouldn't change it* sort of way. She wondered how they had got there. Or, rather, how she hadn't. I'm probably on some goddamned yet-to-be-discovered spectrum, she thought. Doctors, in years to come, shall break the news gently to concerned parents that their young Tommie or Tammie was on the Lil spectrum. How would they react?

But she quickly bored of the thought.

Turning, she saw a group of highly animated lads near her, talking about a fight of some sort.

'You know me,' said one of them, appealing to the group's established view of his well-meaning character, 'I'd never fight with someone unless I was angry.'

Lil turned away from the affirming tones of the guys who knew him and how he was inherently decent and would never fight at all, unless he was angry. She looked out at the passing traffic, thinking she really ought to learn to drive at some point. Why though?

The guys were still crudely chattering.

'Sarah,' said one, 'You know Sarah, in the office?'

hey all laughed again, beer sodden sneering unattractive laughter.

Lil looked them over, the uncouth fat mouthed bloaters. She took in their chicken-breast arms, frog-leg legs, bad teeth, bumpy skulls, lack of chins and one had a nose which could possibly be used to predict the future. She felt annoyed and very much doubted that Sarah, whoever she was, would want anything to do with any of them, despite what they might think of themselves or indeed her, which was a lot and not much.

One shouted, 'You know lads, she's thirty-six!'

Two almost spat their beer out.

'Grab a granny then,' said one.

Lil listened in shock.

'A bit of mature, bet she could teach us,' they laughed again.

Lil disliked the noise of such ungenerous fake boypack laughter, and felt downhearted by how someone could go from sexbomb to bombsite within, what, four years? No thirty-six-year-old could pass as twenty-six, she thought. They must know.

Annoyed with herself for even dwelling on this, she gathered her wits and her things and left, nodding to the guys as she did so, hating herself for doing it, knowing as she did it that she was doing so to spare herself the comments they would make about her when she had left. She got out and began walking, feeling slightly better.

But only slightly.

As she walked her mind turned to Chicken Curry. Lil could never decide if he was good looking or not. Tall, foppish hair, long face, long legs. She wondered what he would be like in bed. Probably uptight. She shook her head. Dear god, what the hell am I thinking?

She crossed the road to change her thoughts and went into a supermarket.

Too early for couples to spread the smugness, couples, couples everywhere, to lead a soul to drink. She straightened as she walked, mindful of the glances of staff members and the keen eye of the camera lens as CCTV followed her, recording That Woman Who – and walked down the cheese aisle, looked at the special offers, went down the product aisle, before deciding it was time enough and heading for the off-licence.

Everyone is married or twenty-four, she thought, looking around.

She picked up some bottles checking out the percentage and the price, highest and lowest preferably, together a perfect coupling. She found two, took them up and slowly in an assured, *I'm just unwinding after a stressful day at the office and am getting these to casually share with my wonderful husband who is cooking for me at home, as we speak* pace, proceeded towards a checkout.

As she walked she wondered if she had heard her name.

She paused, as one does as if hearing is impaired by leg movement. She looked about, obviously having imagined it, and all the effort of appearing cool was undone. She sighed. And then someone definitely called her name.

Lil turned around.

Anne, or as she had been affectionately known, The Missile, was beaming, at her.

'How wonderful to see you!' effused Lil, feeling nervous and very off guard, still eager to please although this particular weapon of war had long since gone from their workplace.

'I knew it was you,' gleamed Anne. 'There's no mistaking you!'

Gleaming and grinning. That gash of red lipstick still intact. Lil had felt it would be the last thing you would see in the tar pitch black of night along with the whites of her eyes just before Anne set to work with rage-fuelled stabbings, richly deserved because the days flattering's and compliments and her job doings had not been enough for her. Lil was happy to realise that the hatred she felt now was stronger than the fear she had felt when they had worked together. Anne was the kind of girl who would murder then make the crime scene investigator realise he had done the deed, and would confess, all the while hoping as he rotted in jail that he could spend one day or one night with the angel who had helped him, before finally realising he had been duped.

To wield such power, thought Lil, smiling to herself, believing that such things – well, maybe not the murder, really – were not beyond Anne's remarkable abilities. The Missile should have sold her talents to some government-led secret misanthropic enterprise in which she would prove invaluable. And earn a fortune.

It was admirable, in its own way, that Anne hadn't, Lil supposed.

'You haven't changed a bit,' The Missile continued. 'I love that retro look, it's all the rage now, you were ahead of your time.'

Lil smiled, again.

'You look amazing,' she managed.

'Hardly,' gushed Anne, flicking her hair.

Even the roots gleamed, thought Lil, mindful of her own greying and, today, very lank tresses. Which she now pulled back.

'I don't have a chance, with Harry and the kids,' went on Anne, smiling.

Lil's stomach sank.

The Missile had landed. She was married, and had kids.

'Oh my goodness,' was all Lil could manage. 'Congratulations,' she added, genuinely pleased for Anne.

Pleased too that such a development must have changed her considerably. Maybe The Missile was human after all?

The Missile laughed.

Lil laughed.

They both laughed.

Lil wanted to get away, now. She was done with the fakery and indeed how could someone's life change so absolutely and incredibly over a few years, when her own life over the same few years absolutely and credibly had not.

'Are you still at Being Alive?' asked Anne. 'I was so glad to get out of there, it was awful.'

Lil kept smiling.

'Well, it just wasn't right for me,' The Missile continued. 'You obviously love it, and the students love you, you're made for it.'

Lil kept smiling.

'And the art, how's that going?' nodded Anne, smiling too.

Lil swallowed.

'I'm working on something new,' she said.

'Oh, all hush hush?' Anne grinned. 'You arty types! Honestly!'

The Missile laughed.

Lil laughed.

They both laughed.

Lil's palms were sweating. She was mindful of her wine, wondering if it would slip. The bottles were hanging down heavily.

'It's been so lovely to see you,' she began, 'I've got to go, I'm late for a dinner party.'

The Missile smiled as her eyes scanned Lil.

'A dinner party?' she said, inviting confirmation of the ridiculous lie. 'Lucky you, I can barely have dinner these

days. You single girls, don't know how good you have it.'
She smiled again. 'Well, you enjoy it, I am so jealous, it
was so nice to see you, I'm thrilled you're doing so well.'

Lil kept smiling as they said their goodbyes, then
watched The Missile totter off on her spikey heels. How
in hell is she married? wondered Lil. And how does she
know I'm still single? I could have a wonderful husband
preparing dinner as we speak! She gripped the wine and
went to the cashier.

Practise bloody speaking normal, she thought as she
smiled at the girl.

Once home she kicked off her shoes, poured a mug of wine
and sat on her bed. Which put the *sit* in bed-sit, as she
joked. It's not like I'm going to get anyone to put into the
bed, I might as well be the sit in the bed-sit rather than a
mattress, which at the rate I eat is a possibility. Another
joke. Also not funny.

She drank some wine.

The sink was clogged, of course it was. And the air
was musty with the smell of a vegetarian diet done on the
cheap. Pasta and beans. Hardly what I imagined when
looking forward to my future, she thought, but then
remembered she had never really imagined her future, so
it couldn't be blamed for not being what she had hoped.
She hadn't, having spent her past living in an alternative
present with no thoughts or imaginings for a future reality.

She was too tired to think. And too tired to blame or
seek an explanation. She took some more wine, lit a
cigarette, stared out of the window at the sky, a sky softly
darkening into evening.

Standing outside Lil flicked her cigarette away. Immediately, Yes Yes hurtled over, brush and pan clanging.

'Sorry, sorry,' said Lil.

'Yes yes,' said the cleaner as she swept the butt and half a tonne of gravel into the dustpan before dumping it into the bin where it made an almighty clash and clatter.

Bloody meal-maker, thought Lil.

'Sorry, never again,' she smiled and nodded at Yes Yes.

'Yes yes,' said Yes Yes, scanning the ground eagle-like.

Shoot shoot yourself yourself thought Lil Lil. I'll even mop up mop up. As she walked back inside she decided a cappuccino would be nice and joined the café queue. The Bitch behind the bar was in full flying form.

'Just because you're rich doesn't mean you can talk to me like that,' he said to a student.

Valid, thought Lil. Good point.

'Do I look like I have a machine for cash?' added The Bitch. 'Do I? What would you even know – the only cash machine you know is daddy.'

The Bitch was flaring and rearing to go. Lil, deciding she didn't need a cappuccino from him after all, left the queue and walked on thinking about the day ahead. Activities Boy bounded up to her out of nowhere, gregarious, and energetic as a labrador in spring.

'Hey Lil, hon,' he shouted.

She smiled. He was a lovely guy.

'Hey love, how are you?'

'In a rush, babe. Pie eating competition on soon.'

'Oh?' she enquired.

'For the students – there's a prize to see who can eat the most pies.'

Lil winced. Death by pie! Compelling proof there is a Darwin after all.

'What's the prize?' she asked.

'A free lunch,' replied Activities Boy.

Lil was impressed.

'Really? Where?'

'Here,' he said. 'They'll have had it – pies!'

Both laughed.

'I didn't think the school's budget would pay for a student to dine out,' she said. 'Good luck,' she added, thinking of the entrails and newspaper and whatever else swept up off floors that would fill the pies to be served, and of how the school really should have copyrighted or trademarked *cheap* as its logo. In all meanings of the word.

The reflection that had on Lil, as a stalwart upholder, she would have given much to be unaware of.

She went upstairs to the staff kitchen, wanting tea now. Just outside the kitchen, she was stopped by Lickspittle.

'Hello gorgeous,' he garlic-breathed all over her. 'You are looking especially womanly today.'

A spot of spittle sprang from his lip and landed on her. She put her hand to her cheek to check and found a small speck. She looked at her hand to find a green dot – pesto. Her stomach churned. Lickspittle was looking her up and down.

'See you later, lush, there's free pies downstairs,' he called.

Further wafts of basil and garlic – normally two of her favourite ingredients but not when emanating from Lickspittle's cavity-filled open mouth – swept over her. Gassing out strongly enough to make atheists believe in the existence of hell and the devil.

She pushed open the door.

In the kitchen Ladymine seemed anguished. His brow was wrinkled. A brow highly prized and much loved and admired – by Ladymine. He seemed greatly saddened, his piety wounded, his peace much disturbed.

'You see,' he was explaining to Hazel, 'The sun gets in and makes them squint, it could damage their eyes,' he wheedled, almost tearful, looking imploringly at Hazel as a puppy might when in the pound and sighted prospective new forever-home owners.

The kind of look that made Lil briefly agree with animal euthanasia, but for people.

Hazel was munching on carrots and dip, which for Lil was the kind of snack you give to children as a treat, after they have been horrible little bastards – hummus, and baby carrots or oat cakes. No kid would be a repeat offender after that, ever. Served with a fun health packed smoothie, then water to wash it all down. Perfect parenting skills.

'Hey Hazel,' said Lil.

Hazel, full mouthed of the lefty idea for reformative prison food smiled. Ladymine meeked up at her, his hands clasped. Even he isn't single thought Lil, probably seen as a bloody catch too.

'They really need blinds on the top floor windows,' he whimpered.

Lil exhaled, and suddenly realised that a word she had just laughingly discovered recently and sneered at for its un-usability and at the overall stupidity of the word and its potential users, seemed apt. For blind or no blind on a window she would dearly love it if Ladymine was defenestrated right now in front of her, just leaving the perfume of his memory to willow around the corridors as he had done.

'It's awful,' he continued, 'and they look to me to help, to change things, they look up to me, it's not my fault, I am so happy to help, but I really must speak and see, it would be so awful if they experienced headaches or such for the sake of a few blinds.'

He sighed.

Lil groaned.

He cannot be for real, she thought, this display of deep humanity was wasted on this particular audience, neither of whom honestly could care less if the entire student body was blinded overnight. And the school wouldn't either, as long as the cheques cleared.

'Try not to worry about it,' she urged Ladymine. 'I let mine wear sunglasses,' she added factitiously.

Ladymine simpered.

Lil boiled the kettle and took a tea bag. She opened the fridge. No milk. She felt like screaming. She slammed the door.

'They always have tea, coffee, milk and sugar, but never all four at the same time.'

She sat down.

'It's awful,' Ladymine continued. 'They are young, developing, and it could damage their eyes.'

Lil was breathtaken. How had a day that had started reasonably well – or in other words as good as it ever got – run into this? A Ladymine weep could be mildly tolerated if there was tea or coffee and Keith. But there was no milk, and no Keith. Just the image of the petals of late summer cut flowers fading in vases in directly sunlit windows. She wondered, not for the first time, if there was a hidden camera and Ladymine was acting it up for job security. A pretended show of concern would be wildly better than the display offered by everyone else. For years they had speculated if their conversations were being recorded to be played back at some future time when incriminating evidence might be needed to get rid of one, or – let's face it – all of the teaching staff. That wouldn't be good. Pretty funny though, she thought, and laughed to herself.

'I'm happy to see you so happy,' said Ladymine, flashing his blinding smile for the camera, his *models would die for your smile* smile.

She nodded, inured to his self-convinced charm.

'Thank you,' she offered smiling her *the cameras are off, thank god* smile.

Ladymine, satisfied he had bestowed his philanthropic gaze upon her, moved on.

'I'm hungry,' he stated, going to the fridge, looking inside and, stricken, turning and shrieking. 'My food! My food! It's gone!'

Lil sighed and got up.

'I'm sure it's not,' she said. 'What was it?'

'Pasta salad,' he said, in a voice akin to a whisper.

'It must be here,' she said.

'It's gone,' he stated, accepting his fate while wearing the expression of a woman in tight-pinching stilettos which will have to be cut off her later with no one to blame but herself and her overweening vanity.

'Maybe Yes Yes threw it out accidentally,' offered Lil.

'What?' asked Ladymine, almost in a swoon of grief.

'The cleaner. Maybe she accidentally threw it out.

Was it in the fridge long?'

'Fresh, today,' choked Ladymine.

Lil went over to the bin and looked in, nothing there except a donut with a bite taken. Waste, she thought. I'd love a donut now. She went to the sink to wash her hands. There, sitting in the sink, was an empty lunch box. Which, had she not known better and been in possession of a suspicious mind, would have seemed to her to have a smiley face drawn into the dregs of the sauce clinging to the bottom. She rinsed it and held it up for Ladymine.

'Is this it?' she asked.

Ladymine gulped and nodded, bravely holding in his overwhelming feelings which it would have shamed him to speak out loud.

'Food thief is back,' she announced to Hazel. 'This isn't cool.'

'It was homemade pasta too,' said Ladymine.

Lil was impressed.

'Wow, you can make pasta?' she said, trying to cheer him up. 'That's amazing.'

'Not me, my girlfriend makes it,' sniffed Ladymine. 'I like pasta, so I got her a pasta maker for Christmas. It was a gift.'

Lil made appropriate approving noises, throwing in some *she's a lucky girl* and such mutterings.

'You can never have enough pasta,' she said.

Ladymine agreed, 'But sometimes it gets a bit, well, it gets – '

'I know,' said Lil. 'She doesn't make it every day though, does she?'

She laughed.

'Every day,' he stated. 'Without fail – pasta bake, pasta salad, pasta pesto, pasta carbonara, tuna pasta, pasta with sauce, pasta and bacon, pasta with chicken – '

'A lot of pasta,' interrupted Lil, feeling newborn respect for Ladymine's girlfriend who perhaps even self-sacrificed and hated pasta, but was willing to make it and eat it every day since Christmas – which had been months ago – committed to making a point.

'Why don't you try something else?' she offered. 'You could get her a rice cooker. Is it her birthday soon?'

Ladymine nodded while rubbing his eyes.

'A rice cooker – what girl wouldn't love that?' continued Lil. 'Think of all the dishes – Indian, Japanese, Chinese, Lebanese, many-a-country-ese, all the curries, sweet and sours, madras, mild medium hot, rice pudding. You could have sushi for starters, a korma for main, milky creamy white for pudding. It's unending what a splendid celebration of food you could have.'

'Maybe,' he said.

'Perfect,' she said.

As she walked out to the courtyard, having decided to forgo the black tea, and thinking about how much she hated bloody rice, a pungent wall of stench belted her across the eyes. She gasped as she surveyed students gorging themselves on vitals-filled pies, bursting with beaks, entrails, eyelids, knuckles and all the other the other bits and bobs salvaged from pig bins countrywide. The smell of gastroenteritis hung like a mist cloud over the revellers. Lil spied Lickspittle in the centre of them all, eating like a heretic, showing off in front of his friends in St Peters Square. Keith stood to one side, smoking.

'Hello love,' she said, going over to him, holding her nose.

'Hey,' he said.

'They really stink,' she said. 'It really stinks here.'

Keith nodded. 'They taste better than they smell.'

'You didn't?' she said.

'I'm afraid I did,' he said.

'How many?'

'Maybe four.'

Lil felt a little sick from the smell.

'The only reason I can see for eating one of those would be for emetic purposes for weight loss,' she said. 'In fact, you would probably never ever want to eat again. Result!' She gasped a little. 'Let's move away, shall we?'

She was feeling very off colour.

They moved away and sat down. Lil exhaled and took out her lunch.

'Healthy,' noted Keith.

Activities Boy suddenly blew a car horn, causing Lil to flinch.

'Yikes,' she said.

'They love it,' said Keith.

Lil looked over.

'They do seem to, don't they? He does have a quality. Only he could make people eat that stuff like that.'

She turned away and began fussing with her salad.

'This seems to be just bloody leaves,' she complained. She grabbed the container. *Nest of leaves*, it boasted, *with zero carbs*. Zero carbs was emblazoned across the single-use killer plastic. She read on, *with all the vitamins and goodness of a pint and a half of water* exclamation mark. She pushed it away. 'Damn it, I should have read that this morning. The seagulls can have it.'

She was annoyed now.

Keith laughed and offered her a cigarette. 'I think I'd prefer to eat the plastic,' he said.

'I would too but I'm hormonal enough,' she said, taking the cigarette. She laughed at herself. 'I tried,' she stated.

'You did,' said Keith.

She smiled over at him.

'How are you feeling? I hope you weren't in trouble at home?'

'All good,' he said, shaking his head. 'Remember, she's working nights, so it's fine.'

Lil inhaled cigarette smoke.

'Of course, I forgot,' she said. 'Well, good. I'm glad that's all over anyway.'

Keith looked at his watch.

'Time to go,' he said.

Lil groaned. 'Already?'

They got up and walked into the building. As they passed reception, they saw Trainwreck appear to be concentrating on something. Lil was intrigued. This was out of character for the receptionist, or rather the Customer-Service Manager and Director of Client Logistics as she had been rechristened in the grand rebranding of the staff late last year. There had even been a ceremony with printed certificates of title, plastic plated trophies and medals of honour handed out, with plastic glass imitation thimbles of own brand prosecco raised to encourage the rock stars of today who were training the rock stars of tomorrow, or something like that. Lil had left the rebranding event early, not feeling the love for paper hats, paper-tasting nibbles on paper plates and plastic-plated paper medals of honour. She was grateful for the evening for teaching her that there were depths which even she would not plumb.

'Is Trainwreck colouring in? she asked Keith.

He looked over. 'Yes, yes she is,' he said.

'I've never seen her so intent,' said Lil.

They walked up the staircase.

'See you later love,' she said.

He smiled. 'Pints later?'

She stopped.

'I shouldn't,' she replied. 'Just the one,' she said.

'Just the one,' he repeated.

They both nodded and walked on.

Later, after she and Keith celebrated their mutual restraint in only having had three each before parting ways for the weekend, Lil sat at home, on the floor for once. A cavernous weekend yawned in emptiness ahead of her. Lil sat swaddled by darkness, her back against a black sack of clothes to be taken to the launderette, downing a wine and shuddering. The taste was hideous. She leaned more heavily against the black bag. It bag toppled over, spilling clothes onto the floor. Lil, shifting herself, leaned instead against the wall. She surveyed the clothes, and the whole scene, feeling that its aesthetic could, in theory, make an interesting painting of some sort.

Turning away, she sighed and lit another cigarette.

Keith is probably having dinner now with his girlfriend, she thought, in a nicely lit room – matching crockery – pleasant conversation.

She looked out of her window.

Dinner for two, she thought. I don't have matching crockery. I don't even have crockery any more. Lil followed the *if you can't cook it in fifteen minutes in one pot it's not dinner* rule. And extended this a little farther by also now eating from the same pot – saves on washing up, time, and, well, effort. Which was when she did cook. Where was the pleasure in cooking for one anyway?

Lil was also aware of the *good in the kitchen good in the bedroom* rule. It seemed natural. Both were sensory experiences, kneading, mixing etc. She was happy to admit she was a terrible cook, and well, she didn't even have a kitchen, and in the bedroom – well, she admitted it had been a while.

She drank more, thinking of Keith and his partner. She realised that she had never considered that Keith's partner might be jealous of her. They had only met once, very briefly. Lil supposed that it was a quality of the girlfriend not to be jealous, and a quality of Keith that he was so completely trustworthy. Lil had thought it a compliment to herself, but was it not? And was it not, in some way, an insult too?

Was she not even someone to be considered a threat?

Lil looked over at her clothes and felt she really ought to make more of an effort. But clothes were expensive. She drank some more. So is wine, she thought. Anyway, a nice new summer frock would hardly be of any comfort on a cold autumnal Friday night, now would it? Where would I wear it anyway? I don't go anywhere. I don't even know people who go anywhere. Anywhere, meaning somewhere she could meet potential-husband-material. Not that she knew how to spot such material. She couldn't imagine having a husband. She tried to see his face. Closing her eyes, she couldn't picture a face.

I'm too old now anyway, she told herself, bored and embarrassed by her thoughts.

And why do people have children? I can't imagine that urge. What if you really don't like your child? It might not be your fault. Is it anyone's fault when two people don't like each other, are not compatible? I could understand, if you love love love someone and wish to have their child, but otherwise – I don't know, it's just another person, like any other.

And I'm too old for that now, too, so no fear there.

She almost laughed out loud at her earlier presumption about the pram in the corridor and the death of art. I don't even have a corridor, she thought. And art – the only art

I'm at risk of producing is the kind of stuff featured in pictures on plates in the backs of magazines going for a limited edition of twenty-seven million units. I could use the money, she thought, and it's been established I need plates, well, a plate.

She drank some more and felt groggy.

At around four am Lil woke with a start. She hadn't meant to fall asleep. She was still on the floor but had put her head down on her mattress. She looked up. The building's fire alarm was going off. She groaned and wondered to herself who in the hell was making toast at such a time – so inconsiderate – climbed onto her bed and put a pillow over her head.

Soon she fell back asleep.

Not long later she was awoken again, this time by hammering on her door. She wondered if she was dreaming, but then heard a splintering sound at the door which was very real. She got up out of bed quickly. She went over to her door. She opened it.

Two firemen.

And everyone in the building assembled on the stairs and hallway, staring at her. For once she didn't focus on how she must look.

'There was a fire in the apartment downstairs,' said one of the firemen, 'Everyone was evacuated and accounted for, except for you.'

Lil looked at the throng of those who had been evacuated, who now were staring at her, all – she presumed – a little bit disappointed that she was alive. They certainly looked it. Very disappointed.

Aren't we bloody all, she thought.

'We would've had to take the door off. It's procedure,' explained the fireman. 'Smoke inhalation kills.'

Lil nodded, having no idea what to say but understanding that she really should have an idea, that something was expected of her, trying to shake herself, to give the impression of someone who actually cared about this fire in the building which could have killed her, and not about just going back to bed.

'How awful,' she said.

Had there been a phrasebook in existence to help her speak normally, with vocabulary and expressions at the back to learn by heart, she doubted that this situation would have featured between its covers. Trying to collect herself, she stood up straight to show civic and social conscience.

'Is there anything I should do?' she asked for want of knowing what else to say.

The fireman looked at her, and then behind her, at the bedsit. At the clothes falling out of a bin liner. At the full ashtrays. At the empty wine bottles on the floor. At a pair of shoes sitting on top of the draining board which she had been trying, and failing, to resurrect with polish and glue.

'Yes,' he offered. 'Tidy up.'

Lil's mouth dropped open. Speechless, she nodded. And closed the door. Cheeky bastard, she thought. She looked around – it did seem pretty messy – but she didn't care. She went back to the bed, got in, curled up, and again fell asleep.

Three

After a long, long weekend of tidying up, Lil felt she deserved, if not applause, at least love. She decided that she ought to keep on top of things and not just have a mental dervish style blitz on tidying when the rent was due and the landlord came over to get his cash in hand. She had gone to the launderette, cleared the fridge of its empty wine bottles, unblocked the sink, recovering cigarette butts which did sort of make her feel slight shame. She had gathered two bags of rubbish which she marvelled at. And had thrown out the last of her soup bowls, which had become surrogate ash trays, and a cooking pot which was too far gone.

Thus, her kitchen set was even farther reduced. Still, she thought, I only need one cup, one knife, one fork. She got up mid-thought to check if she did in fact have a fork. She found it. Result. And blinked away comparisons with women her age. She was well aware and didn't need to be constantly reminded by the evil Nay Boo sayer in her head. She had also found enough coins littered around to pay for the laundry, so that was a mega plus.

She sat down, lit a cigarette, and stared out at the park and hills beyond.

Sunday night, she thought. Why does everyone hate Monday so much? Surely, Sunday night is the worst? For her it was. Every other day of the week – or, rather, of her life – was like a Tuesday, save for Sunday nights. She wondered if such was ever taken into consideration in courts of law. Or if Sunday night was the night when couples decided enough was enough, and divorce was divorce, which was also a great idea – a saviour of souls and sanity and, perhaps pre-emptively, lives. It would have to be a rock-solid marriage to sustain her and to survive Sunday-night feelings.

Gosh, times two.

How did married couples stand a chance?

Not too bad, she thought, looking around and opening the window to get rid of the cleaning products smell. And seeing, outside, people moving things around and out from the fire apartment. It was probably hardly anything, she thought, wondering how she could find out. There was no one to ask. She lit a cigarette, mentally noting to be careful when putting it out, and remembering that the sink was off limits. That had only been once or twice. At least, I think. She looked out the window again and the clock ticked on.

The next day Lil walked into work and called out a merry good morning at the café. The Bitch turned around and hit her with a lightning-bolt glare, thunder-facedly looked her up and down, then turned away. Or maybe not, thought Lil, laughing to herself. He would probably be all smiles to her later. Probably. Or, maybe not. She laughed again to herself.

Activities Boy bounded by.

'Hey Lil,' he said.

She smiled.

'How are you,' she asked.

'Exhausted,' he said. 'All I will say of the weekend is … Spanish girls,' he smirked.

She smiled.

'Oh,' she said.

'It has to be done,' he said.

'I'm sure it does, and no better doer.'

'Cheers,' he said, laughing. 'See you later.'

She walked on. How is it so easy for some? She wondered, before deciding it was she who had been specially selected by evolution, picked out, singled out – well, all singled out, that was clear – carefully chosen never not only to reproduce but not to be within a whisper of a likelihood of the chance of an opportunity of ever such even in theory or rumour occurring.

She didn't mind.

Spanish girls, she thought, and thought of Spanish guys, and shook her head deciding the fruits wouldn't be worth the labour.

At reception, Trainwreck was applying more varnish to her already heavily painted nails. Her hands looked like the type that could be seen clutching a dagger on the cover of a paperback potboiler which promised murder, naughtiness, more naughtiness, and titillation, with plenty of descriptions of suspenders, ideas of what French lingerie must be like, satin undies, garter belts, and probably moustaches. At least one. Probably on the corpse. The moustached victim would have scrape marks all the way down his back from home grown fingernails which had bled their way down, back in the sexy seventies when men loved that sort of thing, she supposed. Not murder obviously. Or at least, not their own. Lil wondered if men even liked varnished nails. She doubted they noticed, but she was sure they noticed when not enough effort was made and sighingly doubted herself. Again, only the third time so far this morning.

Keith passed her on her way.

'Hey love,' she said.

'I'm off for a smoke,' he said. 'Bloody meeting

today,' he added.

The just-newly-born-from-sleep part of Lil died.

'Why?' she accused, before seeing Gum Chewer in her peripheral vison.

Another part of her died. She had forgotten about Gum Chewer. A forty-year-old student who generally sat lumpish while chewing gum in her class. Loudly. Who does that, apart from him? As *him* was older than her Lil felt it impossible to request he didn't. He should know, she thought, before thinking *you can't blame an ape for being an ape*. Bloody ape.

'I'm going to miss the meeting,' she asserted.

Keith shrugged.

'Chicken Curry seemed pretty adamant that we all attend. He had some serious matter to discuss.'

Lil groaned.

'For god's sake. Serious matter? Well, I guess I'll go out of curiosity to see what he considers a serious matter.'

She turned and followed Keith outside.

At lunchtime Lil pushed through the door into the staff kitchen. She gasped. It smelt as if a peat fire had been lit and old men had been smoking old pipes beside it. Wondering if something had died in the fridge, she opened a window, staring at Ladymine and Plastic Bag and Pen as she did so. Why hadn't those three thought to open it? Ladymine, clutching his lunchbox, was deep in conversation with Plastic Bag and Pen. Who had in his plastic bag, Lil noted approvingly, not just a pen but incredibly a newspaper. Progress, she thought.

Ladymine was squinting.

'Ripped jeans, her jeans were ripped,' he said. 'Maybe they have troubles at home, financial problems?'

He was concerned. Lil pictured him wearing a bib, a

big adult baby bib. It looked like it. A big adult baby bib. She noticed a blob of sauce on his knee, so the picture didn't work. Putting the kettle on, she sat beside Hazel who had also just come in.

Hazel smiled.

'Carrot stick?' she offered.

'God no,' said Lil. 'I mean, thank you! Sorry, I just really don't like carrots, can you imagine if you died and they discovered your last meal had been carrots and dip? The shame would kill you all over again.'

Hazel smiled more broadly.

'I'd like my last meal to be Tom from the accounting course I'm doing at the moment,' she laughed. 'Of course, don't ever tell John that, if you meet him.'

Lil laughed too. And wondered what John – Hazel's man – was like. He was an engineer. Whatever that actually meant, apart from money. She sighed again thinking about money and how nice it would be. Forget about a John at home, just give me the cash, I could buy a John. But, actually a holiday would be nice, a holiday from me, from this. She sighed again, dangerously close to being miserable now.\, she thought.

Taking a carrot stick, she dipped it.

'Actually not too bad,' she said, and smiled. 'I draw the line at carrot cake though, impossible, if I'm going to have my cake I want to eat it, no fear with homemade wholesome veggie in the mix bran plain cake. No.'

Hazel nodded her head, acknowledging this.

'I will remember if ever there's an occasion deserving cake for you.'

Lil laughed. Hazel was nice.

'Thanks love, not really, maybe something to serve with tea after the dumping of my ashes?' Speaking of tea she got up and made herself a cup. She sat back down.

'Why are we here?' she asked Hazel.

Hazel shrugged.

'Well he looked very curried today, and we know he shall not be curried with.'

'Red curry?' asked Lil. 'With rage?' Slight hope in her voice.

Hazel shook her head. 'More green, with mild fury.'

Lil drank her tea. 'Well, it will be rice to see what he's talking about but I do wish he would hurry up and korma on.' She immediately apologized.

Hazel groaned. 'You are forgiven, this once.'

Lil took another carrot. As she did so the door was kicked open by the Buddha.

'I don't have time for this,' he announced either to himself or the room. 'I've things to do, people to see.'

Necks to strangle, dead bodies to defile, thought Lil.

'We aren't even being paid for this!' grunted the Buddha.

No one responded. It was safer not to engage. Lil examined her hands. Ladymine concentrated on cleaning the blob on his knee. Plastic Bag with Pen was reading his newspaper. It was two months old, noticed Lil, but still, it's progress.

The door burst open again, and in marched Lickspittle.

'Hello girls!' he shouted at Lil and Hazel.

Hazel coughed. Lil's nose wrinkled. Lickspittle doesn't smoke, I don't think – she thought – I hope I don't smell like that each time I come from the smoking area. If I do, I would hope someone would tell me. She looked around the room. Ladymine was talking to the stain on his knee. Hazel was dipping. The Buddha was eyeballing Plastic Bag with Pen, who now held the paper up to his face. Perhaps not, thought Lil.

'You both are looking extra honied today,' continued

Lickspittle. 'I wish I wore glasses then I would have four eyes, two for each of you, to rest on, and nestle.'

Both acknowledged this with an *aren't you a card* smile, such was easier.

Lickspittle went on.

'And six pairs of hands, not to mention –'

'What time does this start?' interrupted Lil.

The Buddha glared. 'Why? I suppose you're eager, are you, to hear all the news? You are the perfect employee, aren't you?'

Lil was taken aback.

Don't engage.

'Thank you,' she smiled. 'You always know the right things to say, you are such a sweetheart.'

Ape.

Lickspittle sat opposite her, spreading himself across the two seater. He might as well have had four legs. He certainly took up the entire space. And leaned back a bit, perking up his crotch.

Lil looked away.

A cough was then emitted by Lickspittle, sounding like a motorcycle revving on a cold-winter-back-to-school morning. The kind of rev that would wake little children up to the instant knowledge that school would start in less than an hour. With a test, first thing.

Plastic Bag with Pen turned another page. Hazel dipped. Lil waited.

Others came into the room and sat down.

Non-Entity. Never Speaks. That's Literally What I Said. I'm a Vegan.

The room seemed crowded. No Keith. Lil bet to herself that he wouldn't show up, probably outside having lovely cigarettes and laughing with students. She looked around the room and felt depressed. It looked like everyone was on some spectrum. Probably the Lil Spectrum she thought, all odds bodkins assembled together. Are you vain? Cowardly? Employmentally Challenged? No discernible skills, or marketable abilities? Are you Socially Awkward and Romantically Regressive? If the answer is Yes, then come, come teach English, be the Brand-New Brand You, and teach English today.

She sighed.

And put her head in her hands. And looked down. She was wearing a blue floral dress, second hand, which looked like the material had been stripped off a nineteen seventies settee – a settee, not a sofa – which had been stained with things like runny egg, milky sugared tea, cocktail sausages, and pineapple-from-a-tin chunks. And wine from bottles labelled *red* and *not red*. Things from back in the good old days before foods such as hummus, quinoa and drinks like rosé and cappuccino had been introduced, threatening as they did social revolution and the imminent omnipresent menace of homosexualisation of the nation.

I need new clothes, thought Lil. And to get off this spectrum and stop being That Woman Who –

Chicken Curry came in.

He was carrying papers. A good look, Lil thought. It always made one seem important. A clipboard would have been too much and highly mirth-making, and far too improbable to be taken seriously. In the same way one should never wear a bow tie to work. Who could respect admonishment from a dickie-bowed wonder all wrapped up like gussied Christmas?

She raised her eyes with interest.

Plastic Bag with Pen was now licking the tip of his pen. Never Speaks was quivering in a corner. I'm a Vegan was peppering something which looked like an envelope. Ladymine was glaring at the damp patch on his leg which still had the stain of the blot but now had grown bigger and was surrounded by wetness, which Lickspittle found fascinating. The Buddha was breathing, loudly, very loudly. Hazel ate on, flicking her eyes at the clock.

Lil suddenly felt sorry for Chicken Curry.

But her hair bobbin snapped. She felt her hair slump down. She brushed it back. Chicken Curry coughed. Lil immediately felt pangs regarding the smoky smell in the room. He probably thinks I've been smoking here. She swallowed her instinct to say something. It was plainly pipe smoke anyway, or something dead in the fridge, or actually the oven, she suddenly realised, that made much more sense. She desperately wanted to get up and check.

She looked over at the oven.

It was the oven.

Chicken Curry cleared his throat, looked down his Roman nose at the group and coughed again. Everyone looked up.

'I have,' he declared, 'a number of things to get through today.'

Inwardly Lil died, again. She blessed her leonine nature and its numerous lives, but at this rate all would be used up by tea at four. She didn't want to know. Curiosity killed the cat she self-asserted, before she was reminded by Nay Boo that it probably wasn't the curiosity of the feline which had killed it, in fact most likely not, but instead, a premature demise wrought by inquisitive others.

Bastards.

'Some very serious things have been brought to my attention,' continued Chicken Curry. 'I shall not be curried with, these are matters grave and solemn.' He looked around the room. 'We may indeed, perhaps, need the police involved. The attention of the law, investigation by detectives. Very serious, very grave, very solemn.'

He stopped and looked around for his words to sink in.

'Yes,' he announced, or rather soliloquised as no one was really listening and it was all very dramatic, 'everyone here in this room is either a suspect, and/or guilty.'

He shuffled his papers.

The Buddha seemed to have stopped breathing, the sound of his not-heavy respiration somehow more ominous than his throaty ins and outs. Non-Entity's eyes followed a crack in the ceiling. Lil had never noticed it before. A big crack, she thought. Never Speaks folded his arms, unfolded them, folded them.

Chicken Curry seemed content, doubtless thinking that the silence was dumbfoundery and shock. A still in the air which afforded him the gravitas he felt he deserved. He didn't for a second consider it might be more due to deep boredom, inner screamings, rage and resentment against the banality and tedium which was currently being inflicted upon the unpaid all and the unwashed some.

'I have been told,' he continued, 'that Interpol may be getting involved, such is the enormity of our situation.'

Doesn't that sell flowers, thought Lil. Why the hell?

She stopped questioning.

Ladymine looked askance enough for the entire audience. The Buddha, although he had resumed breathing, was clenching and unclenching his fists, which on another day might have been seen as an exercise in the fight against arthritis.

Lil was grateful she had thanked him earlier.

Ape.

'Yes,' sniffed Chicken Curry. 'Law enforcement agencies across the lands and seas have been informed and know of us here now, and are making moves in our direction.'

He paused.

Lil gave him an *I'm listening intently* nod, out of politeness, while she summoned her acting abilities to try to make concern feature itself in her gaze.

'First,' said Chicken Curry, beginning to shake a little.

The weight of dignity, thought Lil, too much.

'Let's play a little game shall we,' he said.

Lil put her head in her hands.

'Great' roared Lickspittle, 'I love a game, me, strip poker's my favourite,' he said eyeing I'm a Vegan. 'First she strips, then you poke her!'

He roared with laughter.

Chicken Curry ignored this. 'A little quiz shall we?' he said.

Lickspittle tutted and sat back.

Time ticked on.

Ladymine, agitated and blinking with bewilderment, tentatively raised his hand.

'Should we get into teams?' he asked nervously.

'Question one,' began a very exasperated Chicken Curry.

Ladymine cowered.

'What do the following people all have in common?'

Never Speaks took out a pen and paper and looked up earnestly.

'Number one: Joah, from Brazil, who was extradited two months ago for double homicide back home. Number two: Pedro, from Argentina, who was declared clinically dead three months ago. Number three: Christian from Germany who was jailed here two months ago for fraudulent hedge fund creation and personality theft. And finally number four: Xiang from China who was jailed here three months ago for operating a dog farm and selling the produce as venison and foie gras to upmarket French restaurants. What do all these people have in common?'

Lil presumed this was a rhetorical question and didn't volunteer any suggestions.

'They're all men,' shouted Lickspittle, pleased. 'Point for me.'

Silence.

Ladymine was confused. Should something be offered to the mix? What did the four have in common? Yes, they were all men. Maybe they were the same age? Or star sign? He wasn't clear of the direction they were going in.

More silence.

'Not only have they all been in prison these last few months – ' practically shouted Chicken Curry.

'The dead one hasn't,' helped Lickspittle.

' – in prison or dead,' snapped Chicken Curry. 'But also the four of them have been registered students here.'

Lil waited for the rest.

'Additionally to being registered here as students, they all received one hundred percent attendance over the last five months, and were graded excellent for class participation, and for the handing in of homework.'

There it is she thought. Her blood ran cold for a second. She had had a Chinese student in her class. What was her name? Candyfloss or Butterwings or Sweet Apple, something like that. She relaxed. It had been a girl, and she had been there. Can't be me who's at fault, she thought. And I've never seen a day's homework in my life.

She rested assured.

'Just how difficult is it to read a register and mark absent or present?' demanded Chicken Curry almost in a sweat. 'How difficult is it, just how difficult is that? The implications are – '

He was interrupted by the door opening and Keith rushing in.

'Sorry I'm late,' he said. 'I was with a Turkish student. His sister had a baby so his father sent over some cigars, but they've gone missing, we checked everywhere but he thinks they were taken from his bag.'

Lickspittle sprang up.

'That's a disgrace. I'll help look, you can have nothing nice, can you?'

He left the room.

I'm a Vegan was concerned too.

'Oh no!' she said. 'What do they look like, what kind were they?'

'Vegan,' said Keith.

'I'll help too,' she said.

Lil glanced at Chicken Curry who was surveying the commotion. He shuffled his papers, rose, silently passed Keith, and left the room. Keith smiled at Lil as she went to put the kettle on.

'Everything all good?' he asked.

She smiled.

'Did I miss anything?' he asked.

'Nothing much,' she said. 'Standard, seems this time though we've been teaching criminals English.'

The kettle popped.

'Oh well,' said Keith, 'that's not a crime.'

Lil groaned.

'Smoke?'

She smiled, made them tea, and they went outside.

Four

Lil sat on her own in a restaurant and opened the menu once more. She scanned it. She decided, again, on just a main – everything was expensive. She looked for the vegetarian option, again, as though the menu for mains might have changed between scannings, or that she might have missed something. Tomato and pasta, the only one. She resented paying a small fortune for something she could make at home, which would probably taste more or less the same. How many variants were there on the taste of tomato and pasta? She hoped the chef wasn't Italian but decided that she wouldn't ask for *not al dente*. Not after the last time, when she had asked a waiter to relay her preference to the chef, and he had looked at her as though seeing her for how she feared she actually looked and how people were too kind to say so while thinking there goes That Woman Who –

Shuddering, she wondered how she looked now.

Reasonable, she thought.

The waiter having gone, Lil overheard what sounded like a three-act opera coming from the kitchen. It might have been caused by anything but Nay Boo told her it was her fault, she was responsible, she liked swollen over cooked pasta. Why not just spell out to the chef her preference for pineapple on her pizza base and her steak well done? They don't like such things.

Rather like hairdressers when you ask them to cut a

nano inch off, and they shear away half a foot.

Why was everything so difficult?

If only there was a key to unlocking communication with others. She felt she was clear in her instruction. No one likes to be instructed, said Nay Boo. She agreed, hating it herself, but then thought she didn't really hate it, being told what to do was another thing. Perhaps that was how they had interpreted it she wondered, maybe it's not their fault. Then whose fault was it?

She told Nay Boo to shut up.

Feeling like the elephant in the castle she smiled at the waiter. He knew others were coming so she wasn't having dinner for one, or waiting for one to appear who didn't, but making it two dinners for one, no fighting over desserts. Men don't fight over dessert, she thought. I'm not even hugely mad on it. She looked at the menu again, the desserts of course did sound nice, but she could in no way afford to get one.

Bloody hell.

She watched the Italian waiter shimmy between tables. God, she thought, Italians are beautiful, even the bad looking ones are beautiful. I'll bet even the dogs in Italy are cute as they woofa woofa their way up and down boulevards, with Milanese accents, on their tippy toed paws like dressage horses, perfected coiffed and manicured. Even Italian dogs are more dateable than me, she thought. How can a dog looking at you make you body conscious? She thought of Italian dogs looking at her before deciding that they would prefer to be stroked and patted by someone better groomed than her, that they'd deliberately walk towards her only to go to the person beside her, allowing themselves to be cooed over, acting all joyful and puppylike while throwing Lil the sentient evil eye of rejection.

Finishing her glass, she beckoned the waiter.

I'll bet he is twenty four, everyone in this town is twenty four. He probably thinks I look like his mother, no, not his mother – to them their mothers are beautiful – more his mother's best friend, who never got a man, his mother's best friend who's lovely in her own way but, you know, and then cue ungentlemanly but honest laughter.

No need to say it because, yes, we know, we all know.

She ordered another wine.

His teeth, she noticed, were whiter than the sweet lamb of God. I must be mutton dressed and trussed up to him. Not even mutton, more of a rare rescue mountain goat. Overlong hooves, dreadlock woolly hair, and a face longer than the summer solstice. No movies are ever made about the coming-of-age epiphanous moment when you realise you are just not hot. Lil admitted that such a movie would be one she wouldn't care to see, that it would be a mirror no one wished to see held up, your own hand held up was bad enough on a wet Tuesday.

She wondered about surgery, nip and tuck. And thanked the waiter as he placed a glass in front of her. He smiled warmly, nice too, she thought, inward death, again. Her hair bobbin pinged and her hair muffled down. She tried to rearrange it while looking at her feet.

'Lil,' a voice said.

She looked up.

'Sarah!' she almost shrieked.

She stopped fussing with her hair and went over to hug Sarah.

'You look wonderful,' gushed Lil sincerely, 'you cut your hair.'

Sarah put her hand up.

'Don't mention it, I have no idea what in the hell I was thinking, pixie, elfin, sprite, anyone of those words are not a becoming description for someone my age, honestly, and now it will take too long to grow back. I have no idea, I think I was having a hormonal moment.'

Lil reiterated that it looked well good, but left things at that, knowing no end of compliments would change a person's opinion. Also she was slightly stung by the age comment. Sarah was three years younger than Lil.

Maybe having kids aged people, she thought.

Sarah's wine arrived and they chinked.

'How's the family?' asked Lil.

'Great,' replied Sarah. 'Well, you know, over hungry, over tired, over loud, over excited and over needy, and that's just Tom.'

Both laughed.

'And how are you?' asked Sarah.

'You know,' Lil blushed, 'getting older, and now with the grey hair to prove it,' she smiled.

'At least you have hair, I've always been jealous and now sitting here scalped,' laughed Sarah. Sort of.

'So good to see you, and you've lost weight.'

Sarah nodded.

'I'm really happy to see less of you now,' continued Lil. 'I'm not talking about the hair,' she added pre-emptively.

Two more ladies arrived, hugs all round.

'Sorry we're late,' said Megan. 'It's my fault, honestly the afternoon just disappeared, I really think I've lost a day this week.'

'It'll be in the last place you look,' said Sarah.

Megan laughed. 'I wouldn't know where to start.'

'You could try with yesterday,' offered Lil.

Megan smiled.

Soph took two more glasses off the waiter. She smiled. He smiled.

'He's quite easy on the eye,' she said approvingly.

They all laughed and agreed, as they chinked glasses.

'Nice hair,' said Megan to Sarah.

Sarah shook her head. 'Oh don't. It would have risen at its own reflection had there been any left. I look like I had a tumble in a haystack. Never ever trust a hairdresser who calls himself *an artist with a vision for you*. An artist – my thatched head. Obviously his vision for me was dystopic. I would say I'm never going back to him but that would be evident as I think never is the time period required to regrow it. The last time I had hair like this was twenty years ago, when I dumped Australian Bob and threw out my wardrobe. Two weeks later, no boyfriend, no clothes, no hair. I looked like a voodoo doll. For two years it was a scorched earth period romantically.' She sipped. 'And now I'm afraid if Tom tries to run his hand through it he'll get second degree carpet burns. Could be a bit of a dry period for a while too, I'm thinking'.

They laughed.

'It is different,' said Megan, 'going to bed with a man whose hair is longer than yours, and having shorter hair than the man you go to bed with.'

'I'm not sure that helps,' said Sarah.

Lil smiled.

'Going to bed with a man would be nice. The last time I went to bed with a man, I ended up the emergency room because I tripped over his guide dog in the night. The dog had to be put down. It, unlike the man, could see. It was considered the best thing to do. A mercy.'

She laughed.

The ladies glanced at each other.

'Sometimes I think I'd love to be single again,' said Megan. 'I remember when I was pregnant with the twins thinking that there was a party going on in my uterus and

I wasn't invited, then I realised, I was the venue, and the next party I would be invited to would be my own fiftieth. I was morning sickened that moment I can tell you.' She laughed.

Lil smiled. The others nodded.

'Can you imagine,' continued Soph, 'having a bed all to yourself, being able to have a glass of wine during the day, going out whenever you wanted, not having to tell anyone where you are going, or tell anyone where you've been – '

They all nodded.

' – having Italian waiters serve you breakfast, brunch, dinner and tea, without ever going near the kitchen?'

They smiled.

'I'd just love to have showers for as long as I'd like,' said Sarah. 'And not have to feel guilty or like a stealth criminal when slathering on expensive ineffective stretch mark diminishing cream.'

They all nodded.

Lil felt eeked with embarrassment. As if any of this applied to her – despite it's being for her benefit. Her mind flicked to the bedsit looming at the end of her day. She thought of the goddamned sink and her one pot resting in it, with bits of yesterday's tomato and pasta welded onto the sides. She took another swig of wine and suddenly wished she could go – she still had half a bottle of wine left in the bedsit. At home, while she might feel like aberrant anatomical matter gone wrong, at least she couldn't see herself as one writ large in full splendour, sticking out a mile within the group. There would be no need for a police line-up, no need for an expert sleuth to employ her skill.

Lil was a masquerading fraud, easy to spot, unavoidable, That Woman Who –

Silence fell as the waiter brought their food. Everyone had ordered just a main – at which Lil had felt relieved – she had rehearsed in her mind how to downplay everything and appear cool, uninterested in food, not hungry enough to justify a starter or a dessert.

'How is Being Alive these days?' asked Megan. 'Still as mad as ever?'

Lil swallowed.

'Oh, Dead Inside, Yes, no change there, a new director.'

'Is Keith still there?' asked Soph.

Lil nodded and smiled. 'Very much so.'

Megan was surprised. 'I thought he would have moved on by now,' she said.

'To a proper job?' said Lil.

'That's not what I meant,' said Megan firmly.

'I just meant that as he's as good as married now, and his partner is a doctor, right? She might want him to – '

' – get a proper job,' finished Lil.

'No that's not fair Lil,' said Megan. 'I meant, a higher paying job. Being Alive practically indentures its staff. We all know this.'

Lil nodded.

'I know, sorry. No, Keith is still there, for the moment at least. I imagine he will leave, he should, he is too good for that place.'

She sipped.

A silence fell over the group. Rather a pall clouding felt Lil.

'I truly hope he does go, for his sake,' continued Lil.

The others looked at her.

'But it's not easy to change. I mean, with my qualifications, and now my age – I'm not twenty-four anymore, or even twenty anything. Who would want this?'

She motioned to herself. 'When they could have that? Who knew that ageism would pounce, not me for sure.'

'Many people would want you,' urged Megan. 'My goodness, the skills you have built up, and staying in one place for a long time looks great on a CV.'

Sarah agreed.

'It shows loyalty, dependability, staying power, ability to change and adapt as times change and adapt.'

Lil shook her head in doubt.

'We did have some insane times,' she said, wishing to change the subject from her.

'I remember getting drunk with students,' said Soph. 'How cringe is that? Admittedly, it was with Other Sarah – wow, she always managed to unwrap students like they were Turkish delight! I was so jealous, no student ever showed any interest in me. She always got them.'

They all howled.

'Nor me,' said Megan.

'What are the staff like now?' asked Sarah.

Lil thought a moment. 'Strange,' she decided. 'A little strange, not good strange, but strange strange, and before you say it, I know coming from me, but yes, I am aware, and yes I think they are way out of my league.'

The others took on board this information.

'Everyone everywhere is a bit strange,' said Sarah. 'But I understand what you mean. A girl in work invited me to go for a coffee with her some Saturday so we could *chew the chit chat* – I didn't go.'

The others laughed.

'She did not say that?' protested Megan.

'Oh yes she did,' confirmed Sarah.

'It's so hard to make new friends,' said Lil.

Everyone agreed.

'Especially at our age,' offered Soph. 'I really don't

have the time.'

Lil put her head down. She had the time and the need but, it would seem, no longer the ability.

'I miss you all,' she said. 'My life is so much better because you're in it, thank you.'

The others were silent for a moment.

'That goes for all of us here,' said Sarah.

'Absolutely,' said Soph.

'Here's to friendship,' said Megan raising her glass.

They all chinked then sipped.

'I want to say here's to Italian waiters too,' said Sarah. 'I think we may need one now for more wine, and I may need one at some inevitable stage later when Tom's skin-stripped palms are bandaged and bound.'

She laughed, and beckoned the waiter for more wine.

'It is hard to make new friends,' said Megan. 'My neighbour invited me to join the Neighbourhood Kleaning Krew – cleaning and crew with a K and a K. I have absolutely no idea why they did that. Why oh why oh why? And why not community, instead of neighbourhood, with a K? Kleaning Krew, for god's sake, with a K and a K. The idea of all that forced, *hey are you in the Krew? Yes, I'm one of the Krew*. All with an *aren't we silly and fun* laugh. Makes my stomach turn over. It's very worthy but I have no wish to spend my twenty-seven free minutes on a Saturday afternoon bagging garbage outside. Probably left on the street by *their* bloody teenagers. So it's difficult enough cleaning up inside, but outside, cleaning up after the neighbours' bratty kids, with a K? No! All they are short of is printing a tee shirt with Kleaning Krew on it. It just scares me. If I ever end up like that, please one of you shoot me. Maybe not on the street though – those cleaners have enough to contend with – contend with a C.'

They laughed.

'I tried to make friends myself, recently,' said Soph. 'One of the girls in work is a singer, obviously, so I joined with the others and went to see her. I know she had just passed her driving test, and had presumably been studying for the past few months. I have a feeling, just a feeling, that it may have influenced her, or rather inspired her.' She took a sip. 'It was a jazz night.' Another sip. 'There was certainly a theme to the songs she sang: *I indicated to you, I'm in a jam, You took me for a spin, I'm getting nowhere fast, Let's change the gear, You were in my blind spot, I'm putting the brakes on you*, and finally, my own favourite, *I'm parking you*. It was quite the musical treat.'

They laughed.

'I'm not sure I will be hanging out with them again,' continued Soph. 'Apart from car ownership, I really didn't feel I had much in common with them. Nice though, indeed, I must say they were and are nice, but I'm not sure friendships at work are the wisest. Aside from Being Alive. And goodness weren't we lucky?'

'We were also younger,' said Lil.

They agreed.

'Perhaps,' said Megan.

Silence.

Dinner had been finished. Lil felt the chill of an ending coming to the evening. She smiled slightly at Megan. Who now seemed at a loss for somethings to say. Sarah looked at her watch.

'I am still so jealous of your hair,' said Megan to Lil.

'Completely,' agreed Sarah. 'In fact never ever more so than now – it's so beautiful.'

Soph agreed. 'You are so beautiful Lil.'

Lil sat staggered, abashed, deeply discomfited.

'Hardly,' she managed.

'Please,' Soph continued, 'you really just need to get out there, put yourself out there. You're being far too selective, give people a chance. I think you're far too unrealistic in your demands. Get out there more and have fun along the way.'

Lil felt a vex of annoyance.

'Get out where?' she demanded. 'Where do you suggest I put myself? And selective? There isn't much selection that I can see at all, and I imagine that any man who's straight and available at my age is either divorced and bitter, or has some sort of degenerate personality thing going on. There's usually a good reason why they're single. Frankly I feel if a guy is attracted to me, at this stage, he must be some sort of niche fetishist. When I'm dead please make sure to use my ashes on the roses in your garden, it would please me to know that at least in death, if not in life, I had managed to repel slugs and insects.'

'That's a bit harsh,' said Megan.

Lil, suddenly not wishing to have her own perspective on her own reality criticised, sighed and looked away.

'There are plenty of very good men out there,' continued Megan. 'And men, too, have been burnt and had bad experiences.'

Lil felt another volley of attack therein.

'I don't want someone who has been burnt or is processing bad experiences. I want someone light. Light-hearted and carefree and who loves at ease.'

She looked down.

'Don't we all?' said Sarah. 'We all want that. Are we that to someone else though?'

Lil was really not in the mood for this now, having the hot coals of her simmering directionless rage raked over and given oxygen, which only served to compound her unhappiness, and make her look really bad in the mind and memory of others, which was doubly unjust as she had not brought up the subject. As it was she who was the subject, and as she felt she had a slight advantage over the others on the topic, she wished they would bow to her superior knowledge and leave well enough alone.

How long is it, she wondered, before well-meaning not well received turns?

She looked down feeling ashamed yet grateful. She knew she was loved. And they were only trying to help. More feelings of anger, but blameless anger. If only there was a villain who could be blamed and vented at, but there wasn't. There never was.

She told Nay Boo to shut up.

'Thank you, Sarah,' she smiled. 'I'm sorry, you are right, of course.'

Sarah smiled that eye flashing smile which made Lil think that Tom must feel twenty foot tall when he was in her company.

'Sometimes I just want to be a trophy girlfriend,' Lil went on. 'I felt at one stage I could be – alright a bronze, but still – and I'm just not ready to be the consolation prize for the guy who came last but at least took part.'

She laughed.

The others smiled. There was silence.

'Well,' said Megan, 'I would settle, no, console myself with a consolation prize – I got the booby prize.'

The others looked at her.

'Peter got a vasectomy,' she continued, 'which is not a bad thing, I'm not complaining about that. He did, however, ask a male nurse to film the procedure and still thinks that it would be great, and hilarious, *hilarious*, for us both to watch it. What in the hell did I marry? I hope the kids don't inherit his sense of humour. If he mentions it once more – one small snip for man one giant snip for him, forget pushing out kids, consider please his huge sacrifice – he may discover himself completely castrated. Now, *that's* a video I would watch. If I managed to hold a camera steady while doing the procedure. I'm not sure he would laugh but I would, over and over, on repeat. Probably leave an awful mess on the tiles, good reason to get reflooring. He wouldn't want the reminder, and probably wouldn't put up much of a fight when it came to the cost.'

They all laughed. Sarah beckoned the waiter for the bill.

Lil took out her purse.

'We've got this,' said Sarah.

Lil profusely fought, but the others ignored her pleas.

'Absolutely not,' said Soph.

Lil accepted gratefully, but as the evening was now closing she felt an ache begin just from knowing it would be such a long time before they met up again. All four got up making vows and promises not to let such a long time pass before they met again. They hugged each other. Lil felt overwhelmed with gratitude. They all smiled at their waiter and thanked him as they left.

Evening had descended when they got outside. Further goodbyes were said before each wended their way in separate directions.

Lil lit a cigarette and headed back to the bedsit.

Five

Next day, she was exhausted. Gum Chewer, it would appear, had started a fashion. So, Lil's morning had consisted of listening to a cacophony of pops, whizzes, squelches, and lots of nasal whistling – a symphony unweighted by even a single English sentence containing grammar, or logic, followable by any auditor. Lil had accepted early on that to wish for both logic and grammar in the same sentence might be asking for the heavens, but was overawed in some respects by how she could get it so wrong. Some of the efforts were so incredible she felt they should be written down and pondered as profundities, probes of the conundrums of existence, insights into what it means to be human.

She had a headache.

Gum Chewer, slack jaw swinging open as he chewed, was the physical representation of a headache. And now peppermint could be added to the roll call of things ruined forever in the life of Lil.

She walked into the staff kitchen. Lickspittle grinned across at her.

'Hello gorgeous!' he shouted.

She smiled, weakly. He was by the window examining a pocket watch in the light.

'That's beautiful,' she said.

'Thanks. My grandfather gave it to me, just before he died.'

Lil made the appropriate head movements in response.

'Do you want it?' he asked.

Lil's head was fuzzy.

'What?'

'I'll give you a good deal. Or even better, you name what you think it's worth, go on.'

Lil's head was not getting better.

'Thank you,' she said, 'but I'm all good for watches. It's just time I need now. But thank you.'

Lickspittle shrugged.

'Your loss, but suit yourself. I wouldn't want to force you to buy something you don't want.'

She nodded faux appreciatively.

'That's very thoughtful of you,' she said.

'I do my best,' said Lickspittle as he pocketed the pocket watch, without making any gags about pocketing pocket watches, before leaving the room.

Lil put on the kettle.

'There's no tea,' said Hazel. 'We've just run out.'

Lil had really wanted tea. She groaned at Hazel, who was eating a chicken breast salad seated with her back to I'm a Vegan. Perhaps lest she cause offence, affront a colleague, or more likely to avoid having to hear a long oration on the values of a plant diet and the effects of eating meat on the brains of humans – their psychology – and of course the injury to the sensate and feeling world of animals and their young. Do it, if not for the animals, for the babies of animal. I'm a Vegan would probably be less offended by sacrificing a chicken in a satanic black ritual mass than by somebody eating it. She might possibly agree with freedom of worship, everyone's right to their faith of choice, and if your worship didn't hurt or affect anyone negatively, why not? An individual's right.

Although, free range hardly meant free choice.

Would the chicken be consulted first?

Votaries of the Dark Lord, she was sure, could rustle up a chicken whisperer who would secure the consent. A votary who could talk to the devil wouldn't find having a chat in a coop with some hens too huge a deal, surely. Satanic votaries on the whole would probably be easier to talk to than vegans. thought Lil. Or more of a laugh anyway.

'Does anyone have some?' she asked the group.

Hazel shrugged.

Lil pondered a moment. She could ask Activities Boy to nip out, but that wouldn't be fair as he didn't drink tea. She could tell him it had protein in it? Or maybe ask Trainwreck? No. The Bitch might have some. Only she couldn't face The Bitch.

'I'll go and get some,' she said.

Ladymine palpably perked up.

'Thank you so much,' he said. 'I really wanted a cup to go with my sandwich, but there was none.'

He sniffed. Lil looked over at him eating a sandwich, not pasta. And what a sandwich. All neatly cut into triangles and de-crusted. It was impressive. As was his eating of the sandwich with a knife and fork. Lil considered the spectrum. Ladymine was on it, definitely.

Ladymine followed her gaze.

'I'm using these because I have a cold coming on,' he explained.

'I didn't say anything,' said Lil none the clearer. 'Oh, a cold, I'm sorry to hear that,' she added. 'The sandwich looks wonderful. Did your girlfriend make it?'

Ladymine shook his head.

'I did, this morning.'

'Really? A man of many skills. Did you use a knife and fork to make them with?'

'No,' he said, perplexed. 'Just my hands.'

Lil nodded.

'You obviously didn't have the cold this morning, then?'

'Right,' he said, laughing.

Lil felt very confused. She had no idea what to add. She looked at the sandwich. And then she looked at Ladymine.

'I hope there's no meat in there,' said I'm a Vegan, laughing.

'No,' said Ladymine. 'Oh but there's cheese. Sorry, sorry, I forgot.'

'We can allow you that,' said I'm a Vegan, smiling at her own magnanimity and wit.

Lil's head hurt.

'Isn't that ice cream you're eating?' she asked I'm a Vegan.

I'm a Vegan smiled benignantly at her, as one would to a simpler soul whose questions caused wry amusement.

'You know it's funny,' she explained to Lil, 'because I'm a vegan, and obviously we don't use anything that has come from the unnecessary and cruel exploitation of animals. But from a human that's a different matter.'

She laughed at her own whimsy and the paradox she felt she must be presenting, before breaking, what she imagined must be, bewildered suspense and curiosity.

'You see, my sister, she's just had a baby, and she wondered if she could make ice cream with some of her left-over expression. And here it is.'

She held up a tub.

'Success! It's crazy isn't it?' She laughed again. 'We're always doing crazy creative things in our family. And it tastes so good too. Would you like to try?'

She held out a spoonful.

'I'm good thank you,' said Lil. 'I'm not a huge ice cream eater, dairy or, otherwise, but thank you, I'm sure it's, yes, it's lovely,' she managed, still smiling as she pulled her coat on, opened the door. 'I just would love some tea. I'm going now to get the tea.'

As she shut the door her smile dropped.

Walking back from the shop Lil realised she had forgotten to get a receipt and felt immediately depressed as she couldn't claim the cash back now. Being Alive had saved itself money, yet again, through her absentmindedness. The staff would now be enjoying tea for the next while on her. It had been the expensive brand too, not the own label. Anyone else would have remembered the receipt.

She lit a cigarette.

'Hello,' said a voice.

Lil jumped.

A man was in front of her.

'Do you have a cigarette?' he asked.

Lil sighed, cigarettes were expensive, but she hated to refuse, knowing the pain of wanting one, and – well, this chap – well, obviously he'd had his challenges in his time. She nodded.

'Of course,' she said, giving him two.

He expressed his gratitude, she lit his cigarette and prepared to go on walking when he looked at her very directly.

'Can I ask you a question?' he said.

Lil was confused, she had given him two cigarettes, she was tired.

'Why am I a virgin?' he asked her.

No, thought Lil, she had definitely not been expecting that. Nor had she any idea of how to answer.

'I'm forty years old and I'm a virgin,' he said, looking

intently at her. 'Is that normal?'

Lil was slightly staggered, truly not knowing what in the hell to say to this, and indeed feeling like a born-again virgin herself. She felt perhaps she was not the authority on the subject that he required. She found herself saying that it was different for everyone and he should be with the right person and he was good and wise to wait, and not bow to societal pressure to have sex and buy things. A rather good response she thought.

'Would you be with me?' he asked.

Lil was taken aback.

'What?' she asked, although she had rightly heard him.

'Would you be my girlfriend, you could help me, you're not too bad looking.'

Lil took a big breath. She was dazzled. How was this happening? Why was this happening? Everyone else was walking on, getting on with their own smooth successful lives, and yet here she was feeling stung by the *not too bad looking* comment. And swallowing her deep desire to pull him up on that. But haggling with a guy who was missing three teeth, two fingernails, and an eyebrow – trying, by doing so, to upgrade her physical status in his and by extension the world at large's estimation – was a poor look and a new low.

She swallowed again.

And instead found herself telling him that she wasn't emotionally ready to commit to a long-term meaningful relationship, but thank you very much, it's nice to be asked. He didn't take this well.

'What?' he asked, his voice raised. 'What's wrong with you? Too good for me, are you?'

And now her eyebrows were raised, too.

So much so they were practically perched on the back

of her head.

'Or maybe you're a lesbian?' he shouted. 'You're a lesbian!' he shouted again.

Lil was rooted with horror. People were staring. What the hell, she wondered, is wrong with them? Haven't they seen a bloody lesbian before? She unrooted herself.

'Bye then,' she said, and lit another cigarette.

Wondering as she did so how, on earth – how – all under thirty seconds – and two cigarettes! Bastard. She walked back to the school wondering and questioning why and how. And then dumped the tea. And went to the bathroom. And sighed.

It would be a long afternoon, she feared.

It was.

But it ended eventually.

As she sat sipping, not swilling, wine, a smiling Keith came over to her.

'Sorry I'm late,' he said.

She smiled back.

'You're always late, it's fine.'

'I was helping a student look for something,' he said, after taking a sip of his beer. 'I have no idea what we were looking for though.'

'So, I take it you didn't find it?'

'No,' he laughed. 'But I had no idea what I was supposed to be looking for.'

'Story of my life,' said Lil.

'I think he'd lost jewellery of some sort,' continued Keith. 'His English was pretty low, so I was hunting around for anything silver. I have no idea if he was upset or angry. Anyway, we looked, but I'm imagining he left it at home, whatever it was.'

He drank some more, as did she.

'Well,' she said, 'if I see anything silver, I'll let you know.'

They chinked glasses and looked around.

'Do I look like a lesbian?' asked Lil.

She looked intently at Keith.

'What?'

'Do I look like and/or seem in any way a lesbian to you?'

She scanned his face. She saw confusion.

She explained.

He laughed, a lot.

'This is not funny,' she iterated. 'It's hard enough as it is. I don't need men thinking I'm a lesbian now. It's not as if they've been lining up anyway.'

She drank.

Keith laughed.

'I'm not sure there's a particular look,' he said.

Lil kept drinking.

'Well, there *is* a look,' she said. 'A look men go for. I have no idea what it is, or how it is transmitted, but I don't have it, and am too old to start looking for – it, the look – forgive the pun.'

She looked around the bar.

'I'm not going to meet my future husband here anyway.'

She lit a cigarette.

'Keith,' she looked at him intently again, 'can you remember your first impression of me? What was your first opinion of me, physically? Did you think I was attractive, or you know, anything like that?'

She looked at him, then looked away, allowing him to remember without the pressure of her peering.

'Sorry Keith,' she smiled, turning back. 'Forget I asked. You really can't remember can you?'

She had been unable to stop herself from saying it.

He laughed.

'I don't know if it was our first meeting, but I remember you were complaining because you had a slight headache, from having too much *liquid lightning* the night before.'

Both laughed.

'I remember,' shrieked Lil. 'I'd been gifted a litre of Cassock vodka!' She screamed with laughter. 'Wow, that was strong stuff!'

They laughed again.

'I thought you were cool,' he said.

'Cool,' she repeated. 'Yes, cool enough to steady a heated racing pulse down to a saunter. People have told me I look scary, or intimidating or a stoner, so now I look like a scary intimidating stoned lesbian, great.'

'Not a bad look,' said Keith laughing.

'I'm not a lesbian,' said Lil, a touch too loud. 'I just don't know any more. The only guys I attract have something off about them or have that undefinable quality of wrongness, something off and wrong. The last guy who approached me in a bar had an upside-down crucifix tattooed onto his face. Now, that is a statement to tell the world, and yet he chose me. He probably thought I looked like an easy recruit to the dark church or would make a good sacrifice, or perhaps he felt by having sex with me he would be making a sacrifice of himself, taking one for the team, getting extra brownie points to move up the ladder, or down or whatever way it works, before leaving me to slink back off to the black lagoon and scrub my fins, knuckles and scales.'

She stubbed out a cigarette.

'It's not funny, Keith,' she said. 'If I'm not careful I'm going to get very desperate, and no, I didn't go home with him, but actually he was quite sweet in a bizarre way, but there is only so much rage and rail against the system a soul can hear in an evening. However much one may agree with it.'

She laughed.

'Sounds like he would have been right at home at the gig last night,' said Keith.

'Oh?'

Lil acted extra interested, feeling she had monopolised too much time talking about herself. Well, fishing for compliments really.

'How was it?' she asked.

'Bizarre,' he answered. 'Some sort of rockabilly protest evening, with bits of rap thrown in every now and again. You'd have loved it – it was terrible.' He laughed. 'I had no idea what the woman was protesting against, but there were lots of songs about fighting. And the wrath. It was very confusing, though, with some mixed messaging. Songs like rage for it, or take a piece of peace, or kick out and storm, or take a back seat. I was confused. I'm probably too old.'

Lil was shocked.

'Don't say that, you are not too old, I'm older than you,' she said, bringing the conversation back to her. 'Sounds pretty awful, but good awful?'

'Yes, good awful.'

They laughed.

Keith finished his beer.

'I've got to go,' he said.

Lil looked up surprised as she had been nestling in for an evening.

'We're going for dinner,' he explained. 'We have a voucher.'

'Lovely,' said Lil, genuinely pleased for him, if not for

herself. 'What are you going for?'

Keith shrugged.

'Not sure, think it is Chinese or Japanese, something - ese, can't remember.'

Lil nodded.

'Lesbianese?' she offered.

'Not sure,' he said with another shrug, 'but if it is I'll take a picture of the staff so we will finally know what they look like.'

Lil smiled.

'I appreciate that, but only if they look less attractive than me.'

She stood up, they hugged, and he went on his way.

Lil watched him go reflecting on just what a great guy he was.

She ordered another wine.

She looked around and saw that everyone seemed to be twenty-four, and decided that everyone in the town was twenty four. A lot of groupings, she noticed. All seemed very jovial and lighthearted. Office workers, she supposed by their attire. And remembered her own days officing, easiest money she could recall.

If I had known then, she thought.

Everyone seemed merry and light-hearted. She envied them and was staggered by how she felt so left behind. Detritus. But then she wondered if she had ever even been in the race. She had never been competitive, it hadn't seemed to be built into her make-up, or at least hadn't been given an opportunity to show itself yet. Except maybe for art.

Nay Boo almost burst out laughing.

Lil looked down, burning with embarrassment. Such silly talk. And she remembered that had been her at twenty-four – talking tomfoolery about art and dedication – which now set her cringing. She looked at the various patrons again and again felt pangs. A good time to leave, she decided.

Knocking back the last of the wine in one gulp she got up and walked out.

Afterwards, making her way along the streets to the bed sit while dwelling a little on her status, she decided that the – admirable – idea that all one needed was oneself, and that a person didn't need others for personal happiness or growth or success, was as dead as the century which had produced it. We are social animals, she argued with herself. But to say openly that one needed others, or even worse a man, would be tantamount to social suicide.

Perhaps it's not all it's cracked up to be, she thought.

She really had no idea.

Compromise wouldn't be so hard – there were very few areas in life about which she was unchanging or adamant – given that she hardly cared about most things much. Which, if she said it out loud, she felt would see her being berated as passionless or with no compass for things. Actually, she thought it was a good thing. Wasn't it? She didn't know, it avoided all the getting worked up and entrenched, and she knew she wasn't an idiot, and knew basics like right and wrong – but then who decided what was right and wrong? She didn't know. She did know that she wanted to work her own life out before solving the riddles of the world, and would have been glad to know where to begin.

She walked along a busy street. A lot of traffic about. And lots of people, walking, on their phones, some with dogs. A dog was a status symbol, she decided. A man with a dog tells the world he is successful, has money, and is in a fulfilled relationship with such a surfeit of emotion he can pour the extra onto a pet.

Good father material.

Lil, true to stereotype, realised she would prefer a cat. Just one.

Well, maybe two – not more.

Coming to her neighbourhood and improving her posture, she walked into the convenience store to begin browsing the wine aisle. Her eyes went to the lower shelves. Obviously the staff had decided that people buying the cheapest bottles should have to stoop to their rightful station, just above the floor. This consolidated the humiliation by thus garnering the sommelier extra attention as they bent down in full view of the standing aficionados before they craned their necks upwards investigating countries and not percentages. She didn't care as she took some.

As she reassumed human form she felt pain in her knees. Extra punishment she decided.

Or was it age?

She wondered if alcohol while oiling the mouth and mind had the effect of freezing the joints too. She thought of the bed in her bed sit, all lumpen and leaden, slumped like a snake that had lost its coil. I should wash my pillows, she thought.

As she deliberated on the price of pillows a girl stopped her.

'Lil? Oh my god, Lil!'

A brown-haired girl smiling in front of her. Lil had to blink to place the girl – a student?

'Holly!' she exclaimed. 'Oh my god, Holly,' she breathed smiling. 'Sorry, I was far way.'

Holly was smiling broadly.

'I can't believe it, I only popped in to get some butter,'

she said, holding it up.

Lil stood holding her bottles and feeling naked. Naked would have been preferable to the floral tablecloth dress she was wearing, replete with plate doilies around the cuffs and hem. Secondhand for a reason she decided.

'You look wonderful' she gushed. 'But no pink hair' she lamented.

Holly laughed.

'Now, that's going back a while,' she said.

'I loved it,' said Lil, 'and I loved you in it – it always made me happy.'

Holly laughed again.

'It's long gone. Didn't really go with the décor of the office or the mood of the management.'

Lil sighed.

'Of course, but I don't see how hair colour can impact professionalism or productivity really. Is it really that threatening or subversive? Personally, I don't see how anyone who spends a lot of time on their hair could ever be a threat to anyone. Look at rockers, the sweetest men on the planet, not great music, but the men are nice.'

Holly agreed, but added that she wouldn't like the competition for the conditioner and mirror, and certainly didn't miss the days of bending over the bath and colouring everything around her except her hair.

'It always looked wonderful,' continued Lil. 'It gave me hope.'

'You are too good,' said Holly shaking her head.

'I was with Keith earlier,' said Lil.

Holly smiled.

'The brat. He's still at Being Alive?'

'I am too – no one else would want me.'

'Well, that's different, you're an institution. The students love you. I don't know how you can still keep doing it, you're amazing.'

Lil shook her head.

'Hardly. And of course the money is the same.'

Hazel rolled her eyes.

'Bottle of red,' she said. 'Best idea ever.'

Lil smiled gratefully.

'How are *you*?' asked Holly. 'Have you been painting recently?'

Lil flushed, feeling rumbled and electrified.

'No not recently,' she said briefly.

Holly looked at her with mock crossness.

'You need to get on that, my girl. You are so gifted.'

Lil's blush deepened – she felt a fraud.

'I would be the first to buy one, Lil. Even if I couldn't afford it. I'd get a loan. I'd invest.'

Lil shook her head hoping the subject would change.

'We can't even afford to get the walls painted now at the moment,' continued Holly. 'The paint is picking off so much it looks like all the carpets have dandruff. It's rotten.'

'We?' asked Lil, surprised.

'Can you believe it?' smiled Holly. 'I even have a son, Fred.'

Lil's breath was taken away.

'Wow!' she said. 'How amazing. I'm so pleased for you, and thrilled that your wonderful genes have been carried on, so a new generation can too be delighted.'

Holly laughed.

'I'm not sure about that, it's bedlam, never ending bedlam.'

'Oh, but good bedlam,' Lil practically cooed.

'He's a good guy though,' said Holly, 'A country lad. It was a beautiful moment to witness his first baby steps out of the wellies, and his first words that weren't about farming or agriculture. Special.'

Both laughed.

'It's still stressful going on a walk when it's not only the dog you have to worry about rolling in the mud and trailing half a mountain into the car. I can't take my eyes off him for half a second or he's gone.'

Lil was filled with affection.

'I can't tell you how happy I am for you, and to see you.'

Holly shook her head.

'Would you stop? You haven't changed at all. You're still the painterly beauty.'

It was now Lil's time to deny.

Holly smiled. 'I'm so sorry Lil, but I've got to go. I left them both in the car, and I'm not sure I opened a window.'

Lil reached out and hugged her.

'We need to do coffee or wine one of these days,' said Holly. 'And bring the brat Keith too.'

They hugged again, and she was gone. Lil was proud of her. Holly had always been a motivated and highly admirable young girl. God, she isn't even thirty, thought Lil as she walked up to the cashier, thrilled that he had seen her with someone, and was a witness to the fact that she wasn't always in there alone buying cheap wine. Buoyed up by her encounter she smiled at him.

'That was a good friend of mine' she informed him, smilingly proud.

The cashier didn't say anything.

Slightly deflated she paid and left.

Six

Lil awoke suddenly, sat up and looked around. She was groggy but convinced she had heard her name being called. Softly, but still it had sounded to her that there was absolutely someone calling her. Rubbing her face, convinced she had been called back from sleep by someone, she looked around. She had no idea of the time. She was exhausted and confused. It had been a very nice voice, soft seductive almost.

Male.

It had sounded caring.

Sighing, she woke up a little more. A full moon was shining directly in the window, making silhouettes of the wine bottle and last standing soup bowl, now ashtray. Twin sentinels, she thought.

Getting out of bed, she looked at the full moon. Solitary and sublime. She took comfort from it, as she knew many had before her, and felt it was watching over her, mute but caring. She lit a cigarette. Outside, it was cloudless. She closed her eyes almost out of deference to the still solemnity of the moon's grandeur, as if to continue looking would be an affront. And focused on the souls who must surely be present around her, almost palpable, but just that little out of reach. Of course it could only be in moonlight when such a realm could be felt to appear, she thought.

What souls would come out in the blazing glare of the

sun, beating down? What place is there for the souls and the spirits among the sun-worshipping revellers celebrating their Bacchanal beings in the warmth of the glow? All fooled into the belief that in the light there are no shadows and such life as it teems and bounds, frolicking in front of them would have no ending.

She exhaled.

That belief was not hers, she knew, nor it would seem had been intended for her. She looked out, very tired. Sure and stately she thought, a godhead, calling its souls. It was a stern patrician energy she felt, benevolent but all-seeing all-white light truth. The honesty of pure energy. A cloud drifted across. Of course. She finished her cigarette, tired of musing, and padded back to bed.

The next day at twelve-thirty Lil pushed in the door to the staff kitchen. She was tired, not having slept well at all. She put on the kettle.

'There's no milk,' offered I'm a Vegan.

Lil groaned. The idea of tea and a cigarette had sustained her for the last thirty minutes of hyper giddiness in class.

'You can have some of mine,' said I'm a Vegan. 'It's soy.'

Not your sister's then, thought Lil. 'Thank you, but no, it's fine,' said Lil.

'You should try it,' urged I'm a Vegan. 'It's just as good and it tastes just the same, but doesn't come from the brutalisation of animal mothers still being milked as their babies are being snatched for the slaughter.'

Lil's eyes raised to the heavens but more in a look of blame than beseeching for help. Even Jesus had eaten fish, she thought. She wondered if he would have survived the days in the desert with I'm a Vegan. She decided that if a few bits of loaves could have fed a few hundred he might have used a whole vegan to feed a thousand. But then she reconsidered. There was probably more meat on the loaves, and most certainly a lot less chew.

'I thought,' said Lil, 'that soya beans were propagated by genetically modified seeds, which are single use only and which enslave farmers, and that farmed bees are used for pollination.'

I'm a Vegan took this intelligence on board. She was displeased. 'I'm not too sure about that,' she said, 'but I am sure exploiting large sentient animals owned by debt-enslaved farmers could not be worsened.'

Oh yes it could, thought Lil bored by all of this, and tired. She made her tea black. She sat down.

I'm a Vegan smiled.

'You know the way,' she began, 'that most people think you're a bit of a bitch?'

Lil was grateful that her tiredness prevented a reaction. She didn't know the way, but instead sipped. 'Just most? And just a bit of one? I'm disappointed. I must remedy that by the end of the business day.'

I'm a Vegan smiled. 'Well, of course, *I* actually don't,' she laughed.

First on the top of the list to gain clarification thought Lil, and once on the list, someone can move up or down, but never off.

'I know you're a good person,' confided I'm a Vegan.

You also know that patent paper shoes and coats made from leaf linen are the future, thought Lil, suddenly wishing for a deluge of rain.

I'm a Vegan continued. 'And I know – '

' – that fake fur on coats is actually cat hair?' interrupted Lil.

I'm a Vegan ignored this. 'That if you too think about it, you'll see the light.' She leaned over and handed Lil a flyer. It had a baby bunny on it Of course it did. Bloody rabbits, thought Lil, nasty feral rats with a wash and blow dry. She studied the flyer. It had all the usual vocabulary of murder, abduction, blood of the innocents, plunder, immorality, and decadence. Decadence, thought Lil, that's a new one. Who would have thought a ham sandwich could be decadent? 'This is some serious quality paper' she said, 'I wonder if it is from sustainable forests.'

The plastic wipeable sheen told her not.

'That's not important now,' urged I'm a Vegan. 'What, however, is, are the cows – you need to think of them. Those poor cows milked every day, from their heavy, over-swollen udders.'

'Each and every lucky cow,' said Lil wondering if I'm a Vegan was going to cry, 'udder with a double D.'

I'm a Vegan shot a look of reproof.

'How would you like it if you had two suction devices clamped to your breasts pumping you for all their worth?'.

'I've never really thought about it,' said Lil, lying.

'Well think about it,' urged I'm a Vegan. 'We can be heroes. They're not mechanised, they're animals.'

Lil put down the flyer.

'Right, so,' she said reflecting that she was getting a lecture on mechanised objects from a woman who, if a vibrator was held anywhere near her, would cause the batteries to die. She sipped on.

The door opened as Non-Entity and Ladymine came in.

'I think we have a meeting now,' said Ladymine apologetically.

They sat down.

Lil gritted her teeth. Another meeting.

Lickspittle came in. 'What's this about a meeting?' he complained as he went to a table and sat down. He took out a pen and paper. 'I'll take the notes,' he joked as he took the lid off the pen, looked at it, then licked the nip.

'That's a beautiful pen,' said Lil admiring the fountain pen in his hand.

'Thanks gorgeous,' he said. 'My sister gave it to me, to encourage my artistic side,' he nodded at her and looked back at the pen. 'Do you want it?' he asked, 'I'll give you a good price,' he said.

Lil smiled shaking her head. 'I'm all good,' she said.

The Buddha burst through the door. 'What's this about a meeting?' he demanded. 'Another meeting – we're not paid for these. I want my lunch. There's a reason it's called lunchtime. It's alright for him, he can have his lunch in office or anywhere at any time he likes. Can I take my lunch out in class? No. I might have to in the future if this goes on. He won't be happy then, will he?'

Lil didn't engage. She rubbed her eyes.

Keith came in. 'I hear there's a meeting?' he said.

Lil did not need to hear the word meeting one more time.

'We have time for a smoke, don't we?' asked Keith.

She nodded, but just as they reached the door it flew open. Chicken Curry swept in.

Lil and Keith toppled back onto a sofa, chastened.

Chicken curry strode to the top of the room. He cleared his throat and rustled his papers.

A dense air of boredom thudded onto Lil. She groaned, dying inside.

Chicken Curry looked down his Roman nose and around the room, which was filling up. He was irked and agitated. An expectant hush had fallen. He cleared his throat again. 'I have calamitous news,' he began.

Calamitous thought Lil.

'Calamitous' whispered Keith.

Calamitous, thought Lil again. This could be interesting. She perked up. She wondered how high it would be going this time – perhaps as they spoke they were being live streamed to secret service agents all around the globe? She adjusted her posture. Who knew? Perhaps a press conference would be called? She might have to make statements, or maybe her legal team would advise her to simply comment *no comment*. It was all very intriguing.

Hazel had cucumber and hummus and was dipping while glancing at the clock.

Lil sighed and slumped.

Chicken Curry coughed again, and began.

'A concerned admirer brought to my attention some things which are being conducted in the classrooms here at Being Alive.'

He looked around the room. Concerned admirer? Lil smelt a rabbit without a wash and blow dry. Chicken Curry continued.

'Last evening, I received this, under the door in my office.'

He held up a letter for all to see. It looked like a ransom letter from black and white films of the thirties. It had words on it, cut from newspapers and magazines to form sentences. For Lil however this was a lot more fascinating than those movies of old. She wished she had a glass of wine to truly appreciate the moment.

Chicken Curry looked around the room and then at the letter.

'I don't know why they didn't just print a letter,' he said more to himself, 'but perhaps they didn't have access to a printer,' he added, not wishing to be disloyal to someone who clearly and self-admittedly admired him. 'Allow me to read.' He cleared his throat. 'Dear Director,' he began and scanned the room to let the fact that he was the director, and indeed dear, to sink in. He wished that the deference he had been accorded by an anonymous correspondent would impress, remind, and perhaps even inspire the room.

Ladymine was nodding effusively, which might have been a compensation for the lack of response from the rest.

'Dear Director,' repeated Chicken Curry. 'I am sorry to have to bring something nasty to your attention.' He paused, then continued. 'But, as my esteem for you, the nobility of your stature and position is so, I feel I must.'

Lil covered her face. This could obviously not be real. Surely not.

'I am abashed to inform you that there are dirty doings happening at Being Alive. Enclosed find what was used in class as material. I hope you can root out the violator and restore the sanctity and honour of the institution. I remain your concerned admirer and servant, Anonymous.'

Chicken Curry put the letter down and looked around. There was silence.

Lil had no idea what to say, but nor did anyone. She felt the show could go on without her participation.

Chicken Curry took out another page from his collection and held it up. 'This was included in the envelope.' It looked like a poem, thought Lil. It was printed too. She looked down again avoiding Keith and his obviously, by now, grinning face.

'This appalling, abominable, wretched fouling was delivered in class,' he declared.

Wretched fouling, thought Lil. She wanted to know more.

'I cannot fathom a mind that would not only think such thoughts, but would write them down.' Chicken Curry looked injured.

Type them up, corrected Lil mentally.

'Such foetid expurgation of language here at a language school, under my very nose!' He sniffed his aforementioned nose before looking down it.

Very professionally done, thought Lil, admiring how he remained mindful of his Roman profile while suffering affront. His offence bordered on melodrama. Perhaps he, too, thought that there could be hidden cameras in the building. He looked around for someone to share his astonishment. No one did.

'Read it out sir,' suddenly shouted Lickspittle.

Lil's heart leapt in hope.

Chicken Curry was taken aback. He looked a little bewildered.

'Go on sir,' urged Lickspittle. 'You've ever such a lovely voice. Honied that's how I'd describe it, like honey sir. I'll bet that's not the only thing honied about you.' Lickspittle winked at him.

Chicken Curry was beginning to flounder, he had not anticipated this when he had been rehearsing how he would behave during the shocked and stunned fallout of his news. He'd even brought a box of tissues lest there were tears of shock or shame, or a confession of guilt declared mid-weep.

'We probably should know the content,' offered Hazel.

Lil was thrilled. Hazel was arguably the sole possessor of a voice of sanity and grounded adulthood in the building.

Chicken Curry looked over at her. He was in a bit of a fret. He supposed that, yes, they ought to know.

Lil nodded an encouragement at him.

He took a step back.

Lickspittle leaned back and crossed his legs below the

knee. 'Go on sir,' he said.

Chicken Curry's hands shook a little as he clasped the poem. 'To you,' he paused. 'Woman, an Ode.' He cleared his throat.

'Romantic!' shouted Lickspittle. 'I love a bit of romance. I was saying that just before you came in.' He grinned around the room.

Chicken Curry began again, blushing.

'Your womanly hips
And vaginal tips
Part as if in a smile
A toe that dips
A slide that slips
In for a soft warm while
I could write an editorial
On tips clitoral
To share the view and way
The secrets of an inner spy
On techniques to make you sigh
And honk honk with yippie kiay.'

Chicken Curry stopped. The room was silent. One could have heard a pin drop. In fact, Trainwreck, at reception, did hear a ping of a pin breaking free, followed by the fall of it and one of the photos from the staff gallery. If she were to think about it, she probably could have guessed whose photo it was. But she was busy drying her acrylic nails under a lamp which had been newly bought expressly for that purpose. The results were pleasing.

Lil looked down to her feet. She was speechless. She would have liked to hear the rest, but then maybe not.

Lickspittle was not however speechless. 'That's beautiful,' he said with hushed reverence almost. 'Now *that's* poetry. And it rhymes. Did you write that sir, did you? It's beautiful.' He was in full gush. He started to applaud, 'Well done, sir,' he started to cheer.

Suddenly before Lil knew it everyone in the room was applauding and cheering. Lickspittle led a chorus of *for he's a jolly good fellow* and, staggeringly, people were joining in. Lil recognized that a whole new level had been reached.

Chicken Curry was deeply confused. His eyes had widened and looked like those of a princess who, having awakened from her millennia of sleep, was told that she now lived in emancipated times and not only must rescue herself but would have to get a job. And that her prince charming, should she manage to get one, would probably have a dad body, tartar on his teeth, an angry ex and perhaps a child or two from a previous relationship. As for her future castle -- well, with real estate being the price it was now, it would probably be a five-room-one-bed, with no ensuite, so no guests for banquets then.

Chicken Curry gathered up his papers, affixed a smile and walked out.

Downstairs, as he passed reception, he saw Trainwreck seated with her back to him. She was staring out the window. As he walked he heard a soft sift sift. He stopped, it stopped. He started again, it started again. Picking up his pace, he sped to his office. When he got in, he looked down fearfully. A photo was attached to the heel of his shoe.

He unattached it.

It was his profile portrait from the staff gallery. With his nose scuffed off. He sighed unhappily. He looked up.

'Mummy,' he whispered. 'Oh mummy.'

Seven

Lil and Keith sat outside howling with laughter and disbelief.

'It was well done whoever did it,' Lil conceded. 'I wonder who did do it.'

'A student?' offered Keith.

Lil shook her head. 'Why would they? And anyway, the English was too good, they certainly didn't learn it here.'

They laughed again.

'A staff member then,' said Keith.

'No, same for the staff, the English is way too good for them and too creative. Those who can do, those who can't teach, and those who can't teach work here.'

They both laughed again.

'Well, yes,' said Keith. 'I got my qualification from collecting the tokens on a cereal box.'

'I got mine in exchange for a four-pack of cans, with one already drunk,' Lil laughed. 'As for a degree, I could give an artist's impression of a good job but I couldn't get one.' She exhaled then laughed again. 'Poor Chicken Curry,' she said finally. 'I do feel sorry for him sometimes.'

Keith disagreed and shook his head. 'The guy's an idiot.'

Lil was still sympathetic. 'He is, but sometimes he seems a little lost.' Again she pondered his attractiveness or not.

They took another cigarette and laughed a little more about the letter.

'Pint later?' asked Lil chirpily.

'I can't,' said Keith. 'Off to the in-laws for dinner. If it's vegetarian I'll try and bring you in some tomorrow.'

She smiled. 'Thank you. One more class to go.'

They flicked their cigarettes.

After class, Lil, not in the mood for bed or to sit, walked toward a canal. It was a nice evening. People were all out in groups, sitting around, playing guitars, smoking weed, being generally youthful, content, and together. She walked on and, finding an empty patch, sat down under a tree. She patted its trunk. She looked out on the water which reflected the sun and, with the light shining through the branches above her, made everything seem painterly. Lil pulled out a beer from her bag, lit a cigarette and leaned back against the trunk.

Two dogs came over near her.

She feigned liking them, fearing that the owner, who must already think she was insane as a thirty-something woman sitting alone under a tree by a canal and drinking a beer and would probably consider her a witch worth the burning were she to add dog-disliker to the description.

The dogs scampered off, to her relief.

As she sat staring a guy approached her and asked her if she wanted to buy weed. She declined gratefully. She couldn't understand why he had asked her. I don't look like a stoner, she thought. I am the most uptight person I know. I don't have that stoner vibe, I condition my hair, and have not yet decided on clothing fashioned out of beard hair. Though the dealer was cute, she thought. But asserted silently to herself that she did not want a stoner husband. Once she had considered going to an AA meeting in the hopes of meeting someone. On the upside it was a captive group, of probably needy vulnerable types who would love a shoulder to cry on. And she was a good listener, particularly if it was made easier by the cuteness of the guy. On the downside there was a good chance that said vulnerable type might be an alcoholic. She did not fancy raising a glass of lemonade celebrating their tenth anniversary on the dry.

Tiring of watching life pass she got up, nodding a goodbye to the dealer.

He was cute, she noticed again. Probably twenty-four. She decided she was way too old for him to even consider her, or to consider that her capacity to consider him was still intact. She thought of the bedsit. It's still early she thought. I'm not going to meet anyone at home.

You never meet anyone in bars, reminded Nay Boo.

She walked into a bar, just the one, she thought. Carefully balancing two small bottles of wine and two glasses she walked into the smoking area, which was surprisingly empty save for a couple who seemed to be having some sort of domestic. Perhaps it's better to be single, thought Lil. She sat down and looked around, this isn't so bad.

She took a sip, happy to drink alone and watch as the clouds gathered.

Much later on in bed, Lil woke up. Again she felt as though someone had been calling her. She looked around, the voice had seemed so real. Her throat was dry and her head was dulled. She got out of bed and went to get some water. Walking over to the sink she tripped over her bag, strewing its contents over the floor. She remembered that she hadn't been able to find her wallet in the bar and had had to walk rather than taxi back. Too tired to think about it she took some water, she looked at the bag on the floor, but was far too tired, it was gone, lost in the mists, whoever had taken it, if indeed it had been taken, would be disappointed. She went back to sleep.

The next day as soon as her first break came, Lil in a mildly agitated state ran to the bank. Her palms were sweaty. She was nervous. She needed money but had no non-expired identification. Her passport was four years out of date, she had only realised that morning when grabbing it to bring. The only travelling her passport had done was through the post on day of issue and despatch. Cheap flights and cheap travel were still expensive, to her at least. Certainly beyond her budget.

And beyond her ability to budget.

She couldn't see the value in trying to save for a holiday. Spend eleven months putting money by for a week, for what? A year of sacrifice for a few days dining alone in Paris, or Spain or wherever. She truly admired people who did travel alone, and wished to be like them, but did they spend every other living day alone? She knew the answer, of course they didn't. It's such a pleasure she was always told, you can do what you like, go where you like, eat what you like. Yes, she thought, it's a nice break for them. What if that's the pattern of your life?

The catch cry of *I'll die alone* is much more benign than *I'll live alone*.

Oh, but you meet people, she was often told by returned travellers who, as much as she knew, never referenced a single person they had met on holiday, not alone, much less kept them as a friend in life. Navigating life alone was not a holiday and her idea of a holiday was not one which should have to be navigated alone while hoping that she might *meet other people like herself*.

Anyway, she thought, even if I did make it to the airport, I'd probably get drunk in the departure lounge, miss the plane, then have to spend a few days at an airport hotel and afterwards have to lie to everyone about how great my travels had been – while wearing slapped-on fake tan and a second-hand holiday frock. And making comments about how cold it was now.

She shuddered at the transparency of the lies.

She was desperately trying not to look panicked as she stood in line in the bank. She wished to appear like all the others, normal and functioning members of society, not a complete imbroglio of mess. She got to the counter. The bank clerk had a lot of gel in his hair, she noted.

'I'd like to report a lost card,' she stated.

He nodded and asked her some rudimentary questions. 'The last transaction was at twenty past midnight,' he stated. 'Is that correct?'

Lil blushed as heat soared, she felt revealed and rumbled.

'Yes,' she managed.

The clerk laughed. 'On the beer, were we?' he laughed again. 'Feeling a little emotional today, are we?' he smirked.

Lil coughed, having no idea what to say, and not sure he necessarily wanted her to, pleased enough as he was with this his wit.

'Could I know my balance please?' she asked.

He nodded, still grinning, and told her.

She groaned as her heart sank. 'Not much,' she said in mock humour.

'It's better than a kick in the ovaries,' said the clerk.

Lil simply stared, not fully sure if she had heard correctly.

He was grinning still.

She stared. 'Well, yes, I suppose it is, better than a kick in the ovaries.' She then asked to make a withdrawal.

As he was handing over the cash, she was flooded with relief. He was smiling now. 'Are you single?' he asked.

Lil looked up, again unsure of what she had just heard.

'I like your hair,' he said. 'Maybe one of these evenings we could meet up and share a saucer of milk together,' he purred at her, rolling his Rs.

Lil was staggered, but she had her cash. 'Thank you, but no,' she said, turning to walk away. He purred at her again, but she strode on hurriedly, feeling the weight of the stares of the others in the queue, feeling she had somehow brought this on herself.

Later, outside in the smoking area, Keith shouted with laughter .

'He purred at me,' repeated Lil. 'Do I look like a cat?' She looked at him quizzically. 'So, now I'm an intimidating stoned lesbian catwoman,' she said. 'Are there even lesbian cats?'

Keith shrugged 'Lots of gay lions,' he said.

Lil agreed. 'I've seen the documentaries, it might explain why the lion and not the lioness has better hair. It's just a theory.'

They laughed.

'Honestly,' said Lil. She exhaled. 'It would be easier to be a lesbian, then I wouldn't have to deal with such men.'

Keith shook his head. 'Yes, you would.'

'Yes, I would. Honestly, anyone else would just go in, get money, and leave, but no, I go in and get invited to a saucer of milk, get purred at, and then judged,' she sighed.

Keith laughed again. 'Pints?'

'Yes.'

After pints, Lil arrived back home earlier than expected. Keith had gone off to meet some friends from college, and she had declined his invitation to join. She opened the door. A letter lay on the floor. Her blood froze. Lil never got letters. With a pulsing heart she picked it up and ripped it open. Scanning the type, she read words such as fire, candles, water damage, ceiling, renovation, evacuate premises. She stumbled toward the bed and reread the letter. Her head spun and she actually toppled back onto the bed.

She would have to move.

The ceiling below was essentially the floor of her apartment. She felt electrified with shock. I have to move, she thought. Oh god. Her chest constricted and her head began to swim. I can't afford to move, where will I go, who the hell wants this, me, it was hard enough before. House hunting, house sharing at my age again, no none wants someone like this. They want twenty-four-year-olds, with sexy friends, not me. Half-images of door to dooring flashed before her, showing herself trying to persuade people, to sell herself, but she couldn't form even words, she sank back, curled up and covered her head, too stunned and concerned to cry. She pushed her head deep into her pillow to force sleep to come.

Eight

This would be a wonderful and great thing, she decided, or at least told herself, after spending the entire weekend fretting over the impending move. She would share again, meet new people, who knew? Maybe the future love of her life! That would serve as a fun, *how did you guys meet?* story.

They would all – the others in the flat – have friends. There could be parties, getting to know new people. Maybe one of the people in the flat would know of someone who was looking for a dream employee? Stranger things have happened. And one or two of them might be non-nationals. Lil could end up living with someone in Paris or Barcelona or Milan. The two of them could get on a train and visit all the galleries in Europe, or better yet drive around from country to country. Road trip, but with hotel stops and good snacks, not own brand. She imagined evenings in, weekends would be less miserable having people to share a bottle of wine and a movie with. She would probably drink less too, she thought, which wouldn't be a bad thing. She decided, mid-frantic-halting-attacks-of-panic, that this was the best way forward.

Change is always difficult but always for the better, she told herself.

And resisted the urge to cry as it would all be for the good. So she kept telling herself at least.

Monday morning was surprisingly welcome after

forty-eight hours of seclusion and pep talking to herself and telling Nay Boo to shut up. It had been a weekend more tiring than most. And now she tried to put the letter to the back of her mind.

It was reasonably sunny, and she wasn't wearing floral pattern. She was beginning to have her suspicions about the aesthetics of floral or paisley. Perhaps they should be retired. Perhaps the dresses which hung in her wardrobe should not have been steam stripped off the corpses of those who had died in them, and just left on to be buried in peace too. Reflecting upon some of those dresses, she didn't wonder if it had been the previous wearer's instruction, not wishing to be seen dead in floral anymore. Lil knew the feeling. It wouldn't serve her memory to be last seen laid out in a refashioned bedspread, replete with pillowcase hat and gloves.

New clothes she thought.

Or newish, only one previous wearer, barely worn, birthdays only.

The morning had passed quietly. Most people, luckily for Lil, did not share her optimistic view of Monday mornings so all was quiet in the madhouse. She made tea, with milk this time. There was, however, no sugar so she would forfeit her pick-me-up coffees later. Not too bad though, she thought. New people, she told herself, perhaps she might even be introduced to new things which would start a passion. It could be a whole new flood of fun flowing in to her life. A new tribe of people, like-minded, caring, whose lives did not revolve around English grammar, crowd control, and people pleasing. She could learn a lot, she thought, maybe one would be an expert on something and would show one's new skills, marketable skills.

As she sipped her tea, the scald burnt Nay Boo away.

Opening her emails, fearing a follow-up email of confirmation of her letter, she quickly scanned the inbox looking for a new contact. But her heart plummeted. Christine. An email from Christine. Lil's left cheek smarted as if struck. A slap in the face was never nice. The cheek went hot. She could feel it redden. Opening the letter, she read it, her arms trembling as she did so. And then, closing the programme, she exhaled deeply.

Her face was hurting and her head swimming. Grabbing her cigarettes, still shaking, she went outside.

'She can't be that bad,' said Keith diplomatically.

Lil dragged on her cigarette. 'She is every – single – one – of my worst qualities. Imagine how someone who can't stand me would describe me. Vain, self-centred, cold, defensive, and competitive. That is exactly how she is.' She exhaled deeply.

Keith sort of laughed. 'I don't know anyone who would describe you like that,' he said sincerely.

'You're too nice, and my sweet friend. Even I'm a Vegan said most people think I'm a bitch.'

'That's just I'm a Vegan being I'm a Vegan,' said Keith.

Lil appreciated this. 'Yes, but I'm sure there are some, if not most, who would describe me like that, and they wouldn't be wrong. These are the things I hate about myself but I'm aware they're part of me. Even now when I look in the mirror I see her face. I cannot turn into her.' She seemed fraught.

Keith shook his head. 'You don't look anything like her,' he said, 'at least not from the photo you've shown me.' He waited.

'I can see it,' said Lil, 'in so many ways, but I'm not a liar or a screamer. She screams, blaming everyone for everything, I don't do that. I admit I'm the author of all my own mess.'

'You don't have to meet her,' offered Keith softly.

Lil rubbed her face which was still hot and red. 'I do' she said. 'It would be wrong not to.'

'I'll come with you, if you like,' he said. 'I'd love to meet her.'

Lil shook her head. 'Thank you so much, but no, she would get so angry and I would be terrified of what she would say to you, or about you, later. She is not the nicest person in the world. She's the kind of girl who if a Molotov cocktail was thrown at her would drink it and demand another of the person who threw it. She uses a rifle as a vibrator. Double barrel – she has had children.'

Keith laughed. 'So, your mother is not the kind of girl you would bring home to meet your mother?' he said.

She laughed. 'No, the last time she was here she worked her way through three assistants in one store, yelled at a homeless person telling her to get a job, and had a go at a waiter for not taking her order first. Of course, it was all their faults. She lives her life exercising the best form of defence.'

Keith was silent. 'The offer stays open,' he said.

Lil thanked him effusively. 'I'm done now, pint later?'

Keith was apologetic.

'Not to worry,' she said. 'I need to think about this anyway.' She thanked him and hugged him and went to get her bag.

Lil wandered away, lost in thought. She felt tired now and leaden. She sighed heavily. Christine must just want me as some goddamned companion now, she thought. Some Victorian spinster maid slash servant slash person who could be spoken at. Obviously, as my mother sees it, I have no chance in hell of ever getting married, no career, a stupid job with no cash and nothing binding me here. Perfect for her. A supplicant satellite to orbit around the burning sun of her authority and, of course, discerning judgement. The audacity of her presumption.

Lil's fury heated. She was almost marching along.

Pausing to light a cigarette, she discovered she was outside the national art gallery. Sitting on the steps to finish her cigarette, she watched everyone passing her by. All looking so young and so professional. Stubbing out her cigarette, turning to look at the entrance, she decided to go in. It had been such a long time.

Nine

The hushed aegis of the gallery had a calming effect. Not only did the library-like silence soothe her, there were few people about. She breathed in deeply. It did have the feel of sanctuary. No-one ever had startling or unsettling news broken to them in a gallery, she thought as she walked slowly along, mindful that she was treading on sacred ground.

Coming to a large canvas dominating one wall, she found herself attracted to the dark and dimly lit moon it portrayed over a stark wooded landscape. She appreciated the colour, the black fading to black, took note of the artist, and moved on. As she walked through the rooms, looking at the works on display and remembering all were done by the masters, she also remembered she had once thought she would be a mistress among the men.

She wondered, not for the first time, how different life might be now in image and mentality had there been women painters around back then. The subject matter would surely have been different. Lil doubted that women would paint men as much as men had painted women. And, when they did, would the subject seer have appreciated being the object for once? Probably, but then enough men painted men as sexual objects too, and it wouldn't have to be sexual.

She came to a large portrait. He painted her very hirsute, thought Lil. I wonder if the painter survived this or was hanged instead of the painting?

I wouldn't be pleased with a daubed-on moustache.

She leaned down to check the painter's name and discovered it was a portrait of a lord. An eighteenth-century transvestite, she thought. Good for him. We both have the same taste in florals, she noticed, although I wouldn't be caught painted in this. Glancing down at her own dress, she was pleased to remember she had not worn floral that day. Looking up again, she examined her reflection in the glass of the frame. Not so bad, she thought, passable at least, enough to go relatively unnoticed.

She checked her hair. As she did so she became aware of a man beside her. She startled.

He laughed. 'I didn't mean to make you jump,' he said.

Lil apologised. 'Sorry, sorry, I was far away, and well, just checking my hair hadn't decided to lift off and launch itself outward around my head. It does that, sorry.'

She was flustered.

The man smiled. 'It looks wonderful, you look like you could have stepped down from an oil canvas yourself.'

Lil was taken aback. She looked at him. He looked like a baby spaniel which had just been towel dried after scampering in its first scatter of rain. Momentarily she forgot herself. She had no idea what to say. He was smiling. His teeth are perfect, she thought. Her hands were getting sweaty. 'Thank you,' she managed. She wanted to make a joke about abstract paintings, but didn't, his smiling candour disarmed her. 'You look like you're the inspiration for a gallery of artists,' she said at last, cringe.

He laughed again, it was a joyous sound, the breath of which could breeze away any problem and make every day a summer's one.

'I'm Isaac,' he said, offering his hand.

She took it. It was soft and warm. 'Lil,' she said. 'Like lily, you know the flower that is favoured by funeral directors everywhere. I've been known, myself, to kill time, especially for those who are with me.'

He laughed again.

She felt good.

'Don't kill time,' he said. 'Time is life.'

'I had come in here to kill an afternoon,' she said. 'Where there's a will there's a gang of principal mourners glowing with grief, holiday booked ready to get away.' She wondered what in the good god hell she was saying. 'Isaac is such a beautiful name,' she said. 'Do you know it means to laugh or rejoice?' she added. 'Beautiful,' she sighed.

'I didn't know that,' he said. 'I was named after someone.'

'Isaac?' she suggested.

'Yes, that's the one, did you know him?' he laughed.

Lil shook her head, smiling too. 'I'm sorry I didn't, though I heard he liked to laugh a lot and rejoice in life.'

'Yes, that's definitely the one,' laughed Isaac.

She smiled. The soles of her feet were tingling.

'Is the afternoon dead for you yet?' he asked.

Lil was shocked. 'It's just coming alive,' she said. More cringe but who cares.

'Would you like to get a coffee?' he asked.

Lil felt like she was in some movie now. 'I would rejoice,' she said, not lying.

Sitting down Lil felt amazed and relaxed, seeing a new side to her, and liking what she saw. Strain was falling away for now and it would be managed anyway, things were manageable. She felt she was taking everything in, it certainly had a very new unknown quality. But then, all unknown experiences were at first unknown or something to that effect. She felt that if her eyes got any bigger they would vacuum swallow the entire room into them.

The waitress came over bringing an earl grey and cappuccino and left smiling, renewing Lil's belief that waitresses were the kindest and greatest of all professionals wanting what was best for those in their charge. She looked happy for me, thought Lil, feeling grateful and accepted as part of the human race.

'Earl grey,' said Isaac.

'Very fancy,' Lil smiled. 'I am so regal even my beverages have to be titled, and with lemon on the side. You know when life gives you lemons, put on the kettle and make earl grey. I find that the dignified way. In the past when life gave me lemons I used to make lemon cakes, gorge myself on them and then pile on ten times my body weight. Not as dignified.'

He laughed. 'Dignity – '

' – is my middle name,' finished Lil. 'No, wait, cheap is, damn, I forgot, but you are getting this aren't you?'

They laughed. Lil was pleased, he seemed very clear and effortless as breath. As the breath of his she wished to feel on her face. The very air around him seemed fragrant. She wondered how old he was. He was younger than her, but how much? She wished she had put on makeup, or rather had paid attention when friends in the past had tried to tutor her in that art. She hadn't bothered, thinking canvas was easier to paint, and makeup was deceptive and dishonest. Also she silently had fears of the horror at the great reveal later. Idiot she thought.

'Do you come to this gallery often?' she asked. She might as well have said here it was the same cringe question, but she couldn't think of another question.

He laughed. 'It's just my third time,' he said. 'It's

pretty cool, and you get to meet some interesting people.'

Lil understood the word swoon all of a sudden. 'Very interesting people,' she said. There was a momentary silence, companionable but silence. Lil decided to fill it. 'I do think most of their permanent collection is pretty tame. I'm not a big fan of the classics, you know, ugly fat babies with wings, apple-cheeked women, well-girthed men beside horses, bowls of fruit, dead game, that sort of thing.'

Isaac agreed a little. 'I respect them, but I prefer abstract.'

'Abstract?' disagreed Lil before she could help herself. 'Just fleck and spatter as far as I can see. I can respect the cubists but they don't do anything for me, very bedroom poster circa thirty years ago.' She sipped.

'You have strong opinions,' he said smiling. 'You don't like much do you?'

Lil blushed, shamefaced and silent, and remembered he didn't know her. Panicking, she apologised. 'I'm not like this normally,' she said. 'Well, yes I am, but I do like lots of things. I like you,' she said and instantly wished she were dead. Idiot idiot idiot. She flushed, suffused with eeked horror. It would be better to just extricate herself, which was as awkward and painful sounding as she currently felt.

But he spoke. 'That's so nice,' he smiled, 'and I like you.'

Lil felt she had lost twenty years off her life, or had had twenty years added on, whichever was the more aging. She was frazzled, it would be easier to go and less excruciating. 'Thank you,' she simply said trying to rein herself and her galloping runaway mouthing and stop over-talking.

Pouring herself more tea, she tried to relax a little and

recover, rewind to before, then start again. She looked around the room, then back at Isaac. He was stirring his coffee. He seemed perfectly self-contained. Slim, neatly packaged. Wearing a short-sleeved shirt that looked like it had been warmed into comfy status. She looked at the hair on his arms, which reminded her of toast that had been slightly blackened. She wished to lean into him and just stroke an arm with the back of just one finger, just softly to feel his warmth, soft enough to make him smile and release a sigh which would signal a need for her to sigh with sadness no more.

He drank his coffee and put his cup down. He had a white moustache of cream making him look so adorable to her that paralysis almost overtook her. She mentioned it. He laughed, the white of his teeth and the white of the moustache thrilled her in their simplicity. She almost ached, to be so at ease with the world.

'All gone?' he asked.

She nodded. 'You're not from around here,' she said smiling.

'I've had cappuccino before,' he replied laughing.

'That's not what I meant' she almost implored, 'but you, well, they don't make people like you here, the genetic pool is more of a spill, splashed on a worn linoleum floor.'

He looked doubtful. 'I'm not sure about genetics,' he said. 'I don't think I could even spell it.'

She laughed. 'I mean, you're like an exotic flower here.'

Isaac smiled. 'Well, thank you. I think my ancestors were all criminals and convicts, but exotic flower is pretty nice.'

Lil commended herself for not saying he was pretty and nice and lovely and loveable, but she suddenly felt way out of her depth. She looked around and wished she could just take a moment or three to stand outside herself and then gauge what would be the best next move, to try and find out what a normal person would do next. She felt like she had talked herself into a corner. She remembered she smoked.

'Do you smoke?' she asked.

He shook his head.

She was relieved. 'I didn't think so, you don't look like a smoker, I mean, well your skin is perfect. Do you mind if I quickly grab one?' she asked.

'Of course not,' he said.

Lil was relieved she could take a time out for a second and recalibrate. 'Thank you,' she said getting up. 'I won't be long,' she added foolishly, she thought. She headed out toward the front of the building.

Once outside she walked over to a bench and sat down. She lit a cigarette and inhaled deeply. The cooler air outside was now sobering. She tried to think. She had no ideas of what to do or what she had been doing. She would have loved a good night's sleep and some time to prep and ready herself for the second round. She couldn't think clearly. She looked at the pedestrians, who coldly reminded her of the world waiting for her. Looking away, she tried to think. Truly her mind was boggled. What was this? Surely not just a chance encounter over a coffee, people didn't have coffee with people whom they just wanted to share an afternoon chat with, did they?

She knew she had never really exactly been in the loop of how normal everyday interactions are skilfully carried out, but surely he had liked her, he wouldn't have suggested otherwise? And she triumphed that he had ordered a second round. He could have chosen the moment to leave, or begin to leave. She realised she had absolutely no idea whatsoever. At all. He seemed so happy-go-lucky. Maybe he is like that with everyone? But, she questioned, would he have coffee or tea with everyone? He did seem very cheerful and gregarious, she thought, before scolding herself. Whose side are you on anyway?

She straightened up her posture. She finished her cigarette and went back inside.

Isaac was reading a gallery flyer. 'You're back,' he said smiling at her.

She wanted to say *and you're still here*, but didn't. 'Yes thank you, I ought to stop, but, you know.' She sipped some tea. 'When in doubt drink tea,' she said.

Isaac looked quizzical.

'As they say, or maybe not,' she said, laughing hoping to distract him from the senselessness of her comment. She dearly hoped he would take over now in the conversation. But she thought, he does seem very relaxed, amused even? She remembered how she might look and wished she had gone to the bathroom, but she hadn't even got a brush or comb with her, and anyway a change in her appearance might frighten him, she thought, as a mouse suddenly in the glare of a cat. He might suddenly feel she was moving in for the pounce or worse she might look all ridiculously done-up ready for a last-century, roast-dinner-and-dance date, while very much looking last century and possibly a dog's dinner, mutton dressed as theatrical ham.

It could accentuate her age over him if nothing else. Again, she wondered. Five years, maybe? Meaning seven, but she settled on five. That was manageable, wasn't it? Except for big birthdays. And that didn't matter, she wouldn't be acknowledging those, much less celebrating them in public or alone.

'Gosh, I never asked what it is you do,' she said,

bracing herself for *student*. He couldn't be.

'Believe it or not I'm an artist,' he said.

Lil's mouth dropped open.

Isaac roared out loud with laughter at her reaction. 'I know, I don't really look like one,' he said.

For Lil this was stupendous, too good to be true. Maybe she had had to wait all that time and all those years for fate to align her with the perfect one, perhaps there had been a reason behind everything. People always told her things happened for a reason. Perhaps now everything made sense in the schema of her life. Everything had been readying her to fully appreciate and move forward.

'No, not at all,' she stammered. 'I'm just so thrilled, how wonderful, how glorious.'

He threw his head back and laughed again.

Lil felt dotty.

'You do so look like a muse almost,' she broke out, 'inspiring all you meet. I am sure there's many an artist who have kicked their tri in the pods at being unable to capture your lambent loveliness. Or sculptors, incapable of fashioning your smile marmoreal, have dashed their efforts, and retrained while consoling themselves in fitted kitchens. Not quite so artistic but wipeable and yielding earthly rewards, if not spiritual.'

She said this with mock arching playfulness so as not to embarrass him, or make herself look totally crazy, but to get the point across. To her he was just lovely.

'I'm not sure I understand all of that,' he said smiling, 'but I'll take it as a compliment.'

She smiled.

'Are you an artist?' he asked. 'You look like one.'

Lil smiled. 'That would be the unruly hair, it gives that effect, on a good day.' She was going to mention clothes that look like they have been taken off an exhumed corpse but decided not to.

'I love your style,' he said.

Lil thanked him. This was awkward. What to do or say next. She almost said it was the kind of style that men liked to sit beside for a laugh in a bar but not wake up to for a smile in a bed, but decided not to. She celebrated her fast learning. 'I did do some painting, oil mostly, in the past,' she said.

'I'd love to see some,' said Isaac.

'And I some of your work,' agreed Lil.

Isaac was pleased. 'Let me take your number.'

'Of course.' She lent down and scrabbled in her bag for her phone. The butterflies in her stomach were beating their wings so fast she half suspected on world news the next day a series of earthquakes all over Southeast Asia would be the headlines.

'Let me take yours,' she said. 'So I can call you and then you have mine, it's easier,' she said. Fast learner indeed.

They did so, she saved it, called it, it rang. Cheering inside, she checked that she had saved it. Then went to put her phone back in her bag, double checking again as she placed it inside. Then took it out of her bag, checked it and put it back. She straightened up and smiled.

Just then the waitress came over. Isaac settled the bill. The waitress told them the gallery would be closing shortly and encouraged them to make their way out.

Lil was effusive in her thanks. They walked to the gates. 'I go this way,' said Lil motioning a direction.

'I'm the opposite,' said Isaac. They stood smiling at each other.

'It was such a thrill to meet you,' she said.

'And for me too,' agreed Isaac.

'Thank you again for bringing the afternoon I had

wanted to kill, to most wonderful, gainful life.'

Isaac laughed at the reference. 'Thank you for your company.' There was a pause. 'I've got to go,' he said. 'I'll be in touch, bye.' With that he turned and was gone.

Lil watched him go, staggered. While walking back she felt many feet-tingling reasons to rejoice.

Ten

Lil was practically floating as she went into work the next day. She not only felt light but that she could stand up straight and meet people in the eye. Her head was far away. Usually she felt her head was in the clouds. Rain clouds. Now she felt most breezy. Isaac had messaged her, so she had reason to rejoice. She allowed her mind to think of him – it didn't take too much work for her to hear his laugh or even, if she concentrated, remember how he had smelled.

She smiled suddenly.

All the clichés were true. Looking around her, she felt pity almost for those in relationships. No other suitor could be as beautiful and sweet natured as he. Certainly not as exotic, he was an artist. She knew his work would be good – dismissing her belief that the better the art the worse the person, and her advice to a friend who had been dating an artist, find out if his work is good or not, if it's terrible or boring that would be a good sign, he won't be too emotionally messed up.

Isaac's work would be just lovely. How could it not, being imbued as it would be with his sensibility and presence?

She sighed again and was mentally hugging herself. Trying not to ponder on the incredible nature of this, she instead decided that that was how people met new people. The person wasn't there, the person was there, they were introduced and now they existed in each other's lives. Just like cake, the cake is made, then it is there, then gorged on, and then gone. It made sense, of course it did.

Lil decided she wanted something sweet when she went into work.

It had all been worth it. She had read countless books and heard countless people talking about the long wait and then finally the perfect fit. The message being it was better to wait. Finally, she thought. And it made so much sense. Had we met before I would not have been the me I am now, I obviously have learned so much, so now I know how to behave and be, in a perfect relationship.

How much more can I evolve with him?

Lil yearned to be better.

We have only met and he is already an improving influence, she thought. Yes, she wanted to be better for him. She sighed, content. But decided not to get carried away. It was early days. She let her mind wander and bet to herself he would look unbearably attractive in a suit.

Lil gave her class a surprise catch-up quiz. A test, so she could spend the first two hours in peace as she reflected upon Isaac. So she sat staring out the window wondering what he was doing right at that very moment. Probably padding around barefoot in pyjamas, laughing. He did like to laugh, which was good. Lil appreciated an audience who found her almost as funny as she did herself. Not an attractive quality she knew but as the producer and audience of her own show in her head she was unlikely to change now.

She imagined him having coffee as the day stretched out before him. She imagined him stretching out then yawning.

I should stop smoking, she thought, it wouldn't be nice for him. She paused and then looked back at the students and the clock.

Break time, fantastic.

Outside she sat drinking coffee, with milk, but no sugar. There was no sugar which was a good thing, I'm a Vegan had informed her. Something about it being a killer and manipulating susceptible minds and its detrimental effect on humanity's march toward enlightenment. Lil hadn't been listening really. She had been debating – still with knee-hugging delight - about what would be the best next move with Isaac.

Keith came out looking ropey. 'I thought I might find you here,' he said.

'How are you love?' she asked. 'I didn't see you this morning.'

He sat down. 'It was a bit of a rough night. I got in very late, missed my first class.'

She offered him her coffee. 'Sugarless coffee?'

He took it. 'Bitter,' he said, 'like my soul.'

She smiled. They sat in silence. Keith finished the coffee. She took the cup and put it down.

'Do anything interesting yesterday?' he asked.

She smiled. 'I went to the gallery,' she answered. 'Do you know there's an eighteenth-century portrait of a lord in complete frock and tiara there?'

Keith confessed that he didn't know, and added that you are never fully dressed without your tiara. 'Damn, I forgot mine today, I feel naked, why didn't anyone tell me.'

She smiled.

He coughed.

'I have paracetamol inside,' she mentioned.

He thanked her.

'I may have met someone,' she said tentatively.

Keith turned to look at her quizzically. '*May* have met someone?' he repeated.

'Yes,' she said looking at him.

He analysed her expression. 'Do you mean?' he began.

'Maybe,' she said. She smiled. 'I don't know really.'

Keith didn't say anything.

Lil now told him everything, including most of what had been said and how it had been received. She anxiously examined his reactions.

'What do you think?' she asked finally.

Keith sat back a little. 'This sounds good,' he said. 'He sounds like a nice guy.'

'But, what do you think?' she pressed.

He took a moment. 'It sounds pretty amazing, he's an artist you are an artist, he said he liked your style – you have great style by the way – it sounds promising.'

Lil wasn't sure if this was enough. 'You wouldn't ask a girl for a coffee if you didn't like her, would you?' she said.

'Hell no,' said Keith. 'God no, you wouldn't even talk to her really if you weren't interested, unless you had to.'

Lil nodded, still unsure. 'What if you were just being polite or friendly?'

Keith agreed. 'Well, that *is* possible, but you still wouldn't ask her for a coffee.'

Lil said she didn't think so. 'But what if you were being polite and friendly and from another country and needed friends?' she asked.

Keith reflected on this. 'No, still wouldn't ask a girl I wasn't into to go for a coffee – too complicated. I'd go to a bar.'

Lil took this on board and agreed that such would seem the more natural way of doing things, but then added what in the hell did she know anyway. It seemed complicated to her now. She bemoaned the complexity of the situation and its not being clear enough for her.

'He did message me to meet again,' she said as though trying to convince Keith.

'Which is excellent,' said Keith. 'And no, there's no way a guy would ask to meet a girl he wasn't into for a second time. Not a chance in hell.'

Lil smiled. 'But I took his number,' she said.

'And he messaged you,' said Keith.

Now she was talking about it, it all seemed a bit unreal to her. 'I don't know,' she said finally.

Keith had perked up. 'Sounds to me like you have a date,' he said. 'This is great, Lil.' He whooped for her.

She shushed him, embarrassed, but was pleased. 'Maybe,' she said. 'It does sound like it.'

Keith nodded. His was the kind of delight that Lil feared might wish to broadcast and cheerily tell the world.

'Don't mention this to anyone,' she urged.

He shook his head, and smiled. 'A date, save the date, what's today's date, we know not the hour or the date. Except on this occasion we do know the date.'

She laughed. 'Thank you loveliness,' she said, and then realised something. 'People, well, they often kiss on the first date, don't they?'

'Not always,' he said. 'I'm not sure I did, can't remember.'

Lil seemed perplexed. 'I don't know how things work now – it's been a while. Everyone I know met their partner years ago, when they were much younger than I am now, and it was much easier. Well, not much younger, a premature baby's teeny tiny handful of years younger than I am now, I'm not sure of what I should do. Is it slower now? Or faster? I have absolutely no idea. Should I do something?' She looked at Keith for answers.

'Just relax,' he said, 'and go with it.'

This wasn't quite the reassurance she had been hoping for, though at least he hadn't told her to just be herself.

'Just relax,' he repeated, 'and be yourself, and it'll work itself out.'

This did not help. When did things just work themselves out? She imagined mathematicians, saying 'Oh let's go and have lunch, leave it, just leave that equation, it'll work itself out.' Lil felt anxious now, without clear direction.

'He's younger than me too,' said Lil with heavy reluctance but feeling she had to let Keith know, lest this information was a complete game changer.

'Younger?' asked Keith.

'Five or six years,' said Lil trying to downplay what was huge in her mind.

'How old are you again?' asked Keith.

'Late twenties,' said Lil.

He looked a little disbelieving.

'Mid-thirties, could, I'm sure, still count or be understood as very being late twenties,' she said. 'Late twenties, early thirties, early mid-thirties, they're all interchangeable terms these days,' she said, laughing now.

'Well you don't look a day older,' he said.

'Thank you,' she said laughing again. 'Just to confirm, there's no way a guy would ask to meet up if he wasn't interested?'

'No,' confirmed Keith.

She smiled.

He lit another cigarette. 'So, Tom the cat is on the prowl – '

Lil was listening.

' – and he sees this amazing beautiful tabby, the cat of

his dreams, a cat so beautiful she should be painted and hung on the walls of pyramids. He approaches her slowly, but when she sees him she sits up and extends a paw. Hold it right there Tom, she says, before you come any further you should know I'm a lesbian. Tom stops, he's devastated. A lesbian? he says, A lesbian? Are you kitten me?'

Lil groaned.

Keith laughed.

She lit up. 'So this kiss,' she said. 'God, I'm talking like a fourteen-year-old, long ago before I was a virgin. I'm not so experienced, but should I expect one?'

Keith looked at her. 'I don't know, but you will, the right moment will come' he said, 'and it will be the right moment and the right thing to do.'

Lil digested this. 'The right moment.' This was clear, a breakthrough, almost. It didn't have to be pelting with rain, or to be Christmas by candlelight, or to follow any protocol – just, to be the right moment. This was a relief, which resonated. 'Thank you so much Keith,' she said, 'I feel better now.'

She hugged him. 'The right moment for both of us, right?'

Keith groaned. 'Yes,' he said, 'yes, now let's get another cup of that rotten coffee.'

Lil spent the rest of the afternoon doing an inventory of her appearance. She decided that the size of her chin and forehead combined was actually bigger than the rest of her entire face. She felt that the airport could use her forehead as an extra landing strip during summer peak and her chin as a runway for take-off.

She wondered if her lines were visible, and wondered if makeup should be a consideration. She had never used any before, really and truly never feeling the need, nor having the occasion to. She wasn't skilled, she thought diplomatically, in its application. The trick was to look natural and not like some glazed tart just fresh out of the oven. She wasn't sure if men really liked it or not and regretted not asking Keith. Women wore makeup as empowering and for themselves, or so she had been told. So, not too much, she thought, no-one likes clown face, or being reminded that Halloween was two months ago. It's so hard to know. Not looking tired would be a mega plus, just fresh. She decided she would investigate.

She wondered on her style. Isaac had said he liked it. Which meant to her that it had stood out and he'd noticed it, so, of course, he'd had to say something about it and something polite. If her style was actually in fact great he wouldn't have noticed it and wouldn't have had to say something. Men don't generally notice clothes, she thought, unless what you're wearing is screamingly not unnoticeable.

She thought of her wardrobe. Changing it would be a big task.. She had begun to think that she dressed like a nineteen-seventies semi-detached suburban house. Her clothes, she appraised, had patterns like carpet, wallpaper, settees not sofas and arm chairs, tea cups and cosies, kitchen tiles, bathroom toilet seat covers, toilet roll covers, blankets, bed sheets, draught excluders, even the goddamned copied prints hanging over fireplaces. She needed to upgrade her clothes situation, fast. This could be expensive, but slowly it could be done and imperceptibly transform. She made a mental note by banning any further floral purchases. The strength of her decision was almost transformation enough.

As she walked, she paid attention to the makeup situations on the girls walking by.

Too much. Way too much. So much. Radiating so much, very useful to have if needing to change a tyre on a dark country road on a dark and stormy night. A tiny amount, nice, flattering.

Most seemed not to be wearing any at all, or weren't they?

She stopped outside Mr. Mac Bucket O'Bargains, a bric-a-brac shop of tat and trash. Rubbish at a good price. She went in, sure she had seen makeup there before. It was the kind of shop where socks hung beside garden tools, household products beside biscuits, beauty products beside stationery, and all other odds and sods lumped together. It was the kind of place Lil appreciated. And it was cheap.

She walked along the aisles and came to the cosmetic section, or shelf rather. She took a breath and scanned the products.

All incredibly shiny, she thought, very plastic-looking. Taking up a foundation bottle, she looked at the colour. She had no idea of her shade of white. Grubby-looking wasn't a shade. Nor nicotine either. She looked at the bottle being very unsure. What, she wondered, if I have a reaction to it, what if it just sits on my face, or burns the hell out of me, or runs in the rain?

Can it be so good if it's this cheap?

She looked on the shelf below. There was a serious amount of pinks and blues, and glittery sparkle. She dismissed immediately the glitter, not wishing to look like the rear end of a disco donkey piñata. At least not at the moment. She examined further and then flushed with embarrassment and fear. She realised she must be in the children's make up section – that would explain things. She saw a sales assistant and went over to her.

'Excuse me,' she said.

'Yes,' snapped the assistant, clearly vexed at being interrupted.

'I'm sorry,' said Lil, 'could you tell me if this makeup is for children?'

The assistant looked her up and down. 'I wouldn't be giving makeup to kids,' she said, stared briefly at Lil before resuming what she'd been doing.

Well you are a sweetheart, thought Lil, I hadn't realised I had asked for expert paediatric insight into the benefits and possible dangers of introducing infants to cosmetics.

'Face paint's over there,' pointed the assistant. Lil nodded.

Putting the foundation down she left the shop.

Walking along the street, silently fuming over the sales assistant, she now wanted and – she decided - needed make up and could not possibly go back to the bedsit without anything, something. Coming to a department store, she decided to go in and check it out. The air inside was very fresh and gusty. She inhaled deeply, thinking that the owners must put oxygen in the air conditioning to keep customers in, energised and buying.

She felt sprightlier herself all of a sudden. She looked at the store directory, went to the makeup area and walked in. It was vast, clinical, perfumed. And swarming with very wealthy, very made-up ladies. Lil tried to act natural. She already knew she looked natural, couldn't be more natural, with unmade-up skin and hair loose and free like a brown bear Christmas cub discovering its first spring.

She looked at the walls and walls of products.

This was very much out of her depth. She decided to ask an assistant for help. She would say she was here for a friend who needed a light foundation, for sensitive skin – best to go with that, it should cover all fears – and who also needed a little few extras to match with it. That seemed plausible. She rehearsed it mentally and walked over to the customer service point. She smiled as she walked.

When she got there, she smiled at the assistant. He looks stern, she thought, and began.

'Hello, I'm so sorry I'm here for – '

He interrupted. 'Yes, I know,' he said clearly tired and heated.

Lil was confused.

'You *are* a little late, but we held your spot. We don't normally but please try and be on time, people wait for weeks for a free slot.'

Lil looked behind her to see if there was someone there to whom he was in fact talking. There wasn't. 'Excuse me,' she said, 'I'm sorry, I'm not sure I understand.'

The assistant looked her up and down. 'The makeover, you said you were here for our makeup makeover didn't you? We held your slot.'

Lil stopped breathing. I look like I need a makeover? I'm the before, dear good god. She was horror stricken.

The assistant suspected by her look of shock and pain which would register on a childbirth scale that perhaps he had got it wrong somehow. 'You are here for the makeup makeover?' he asked very, very slowly.

Lil couldn't speak 'I obviously need one,' she said at last. 'Call an ambulance, it's an emergency makeover required, but I was here to buy something, for a friend.' She was flushed and actually wanted to cry.

The assistant by now was horrified too. 'I'm so sorry I thought you said you were here for – '

Lil started to shake her head. 'Don't worry, it's a misunderstanding, these things happen, you must be very busy, thank you for your time, I'm going to go.'

The assistant was deeply apologetic, again. 'Wait here a moment,' he said, going away.

Lil began to cool down and see the funny side of things. Sort of. Well, what crazy, scary, and intimidating stoned lesbian cat lady wouldn't need a makeover?

The assistant came back. 'Here,' he offered her a small branded bag tied with ribbon. 'I shouldn't do this, if anyone asks I didn't give you this. It's a gift bag, free when you spend over a hundred, it has lots and lots of samples, it should keep you going for months. I'm *so* sorry again – it's been hectic in here.' He smiled.

'Thank you so much,' Lil said, wanting to cry again, 'Thank you!'

He smiled. 'Enjoy,' he said, before adding, 'I love your style.'

She glowed. 'And I yours, you're beautiful.' After further effusions she left and went back outside filled with glee and gladness thinking gay men were the greatest people on the planet. He also said he liked my style, she thought, how lovely.

Eleven

Lil walked along insulated with knee-hugging gladness. She felt tall and proud as she walked, thinking this is how other people must feel, normal people. She was happy to be accepted into the human race.

Her mind was filled with the image of Isaac as she walked. She rested on his image, thoughts of meadows of wildflowers, a fiasco of puppies frolicking, even the whoosh of the ocean, entered her mind.

She was thankful no one could hear her. She was in danger of becoming cheerful. She was even enjoying the sun. She silenced Nay Boo who had reminded her of her sunstroke after spending just one hour in the sun once. It had been blazing, she thought, and I was right under it. Or the time when she had received a tropical spider bite after merely twenty minutes on the grass in a park. She had spent two days in a hallucinatory fever taking paracetamol, prescribed by a doctor who told had her that he had never seen a leg so badly poisoned in his life. Helpful. Perhaps a photo? Finally get your name in that medical journal? And oh, the bite's on the other leg. The big red swollen, hot to the touch with bumpy mottled lumps, one. Those are just my varicose veins you're currently admiring.

She was strolling now, and not letting her nervousness take control. There was nothing to be nervous about, normal people do this every day of the week. She didn't even entertain the what if he doesn't show up thoughts.

Feeling relaxed, for once, she arrived at the gates of the park. It was hot. She was wearing factor one hundred. Well, she had applied factor fifty twice, so logically, it adds up. As does sun exposure, in years, twenty minutes in the sun meant ten on her face, and quite frankly no amount of vitamin D would compensate for that, at all. She was early, she thought. As she mentally re-examined her appearance, no floral patterns.

Hearing her name, she turned around but couldn't see him. Suddenly, he appeared, popping out from behind a tree. She smiled, suffused with pleasure at seeing him and incredulity that he was here to see her.

'How lovely to see you,' she said.

'Good to see you too,' he replied. He extended a cardboard cup. 'I got you an earl grey. They had no lemon, so I got for you instead some lemon drizzle cake.' He smiled.

Lil was beyond impressed. 'Wow, thank you.'

He simply laughed again. There it was, that carefree laugh.

Lil wasn't sure of what to say so stayed quiet, so as not to ruin things.

Isaac, animated, looked around, taking everything in. He seemed playful and shiny.

'This is so nice,' she said at last.

'Fantastic,' he agreed.

'I miss the sun.' Lil let her mind dwell on the image of his face, with his hushed brown eyes and feathered spiky hair, standing in tufty irregularity. It was a candid and open face, one which, it seemed, would blanch at even the idea of wrongdoing or unkindness. Such things seemed beyond his ken or comprehension of the world. She wished to be so, but jaded was her middle name, after cheap.

Some had double-barrel surnames, she had double-middle names, maybe triple, she wondered what her third middle name could be. As she was pondering thus Isaac asked her if she would like to sit down. 'Absolutely' she said, they walked to a patch of grass.

'Here?' he asked.

'Perfect,' she replied.

She sipped her tea and watched him. He didn't notice as he was busy being very distracted by the world around him. Lil felt that if a butterfly appeared he would chase after it, ambling across fields in light pursuit until another distraction should side-track him. She wished she could see the world through his eyes. It had already improved to her in their reflection.

Perhaps, I have too, she wondered.

He put his arms behind his head and lay back on the grass. As he did so his tee shirt climbed a little to reveal a glancing of midriff.

She audibly gasped and her heart somersaulted a little. She immediately looked away. She let its beat calm down before returning to look at him.

He sat up, the tee shirt slipped down again. She was relieved but thought of the image, and of how soft and fragrant his skin looked. She pushed aside self-lacerating thoughts of how hers would be by comparison, should they ever be side by side. The sun shone on.

'Some tunes would be nice,' he said.

Lil couldn't have disagreed more – the last thing she wanted was a stereo tsking out some unintelligible tune – but agreed with him, to appear agreeable.

'What kind of music do you like? she added.

'Everything,' he said, 'from cheesy pop to world.'

Lil nodded. 'I don't know much about world music, or indeed the world. I haven't travelled much – the only travelling I've really done is through books.'

Isaac laughed. 'Travelling is the best. You should get out there and see the world.'

She nodded. 'Does it live up to the reviews?' she asked.

'You need to travel more,' he said.

Lil thought of her out-of-date passport and depleted bank account. 'Yes,' she said agreeing. 'But it's so important who you travel with, you need a good travelling companion.'

Isaac agreed. 'But you meet people when you travel,' he said.

Lil sighed. 'I meet people every day,' she said. 'I don't need to travel for that.' He smiled and looked at her.

'I met you,' he said.

Lil felt warmed. 'And how lucky am I, and yet I didn't travel, the world came to me.' She smiled. 'When's your birthday?' she asked.

'April 8th,' he answered looking confused.

Lil looked thoughtful. 'April 8th,' she said. 'A very auspicious date.'

'Why?' he asked, as she had known he would.

'Because you were born,' she said.

Isaac gave an embarrassed yet happy sigh. He looked down and then out beyond them.

Lil leaned back into her thoughts. She had no idea what to think now at this stage. Were things going in her favour? What direction was the conversation going in? She was lost. She looked over at Isaac. He was busy people-watching. Was he so confident, or lazy, or shy that he could just sit and observe? She didn't know. Her experience in such situations was not particularly extensive.

He caught her eye and smiled.

For her it was blinding, she was affirmed by simply sitting and imbibing his sublime. She stopped her mind from racing – surely there was no rush – Keith had mentioned the right time – wasn't it enough just to be there, with him, and have him see and acknowledge her?

She closed her eyes feeling the warmth and seeing his face as it filled her mind's eye.

'I almost forgot,' he said waking her from her reverie. 'I have photos, you did want to see some of my work, didn't you?'

'Absolutely,' she said, and welcomed the excuse to move in closer to him. 'I'm sure they must be beautiful,' she said.

'Don't be,' he said smiling.

'I'm sure so,' she said. 'They are, after all, an extension of who you are. I never separate the artist from the art, so they must be beautiful,' she said. 'I know it's an old-fashioned idea, but I have no interest in art or literature produced from what I understand is a polluted mind.'

Isaac thought about this. 'Some of the best work in the world was done by what may be seen as polluted people. And what do you mean by polluted? One man's symphony is another man's noise pollution. Polluted could be a strong word.'

Lil felt a little criticised, almost.

'I mean, done by someone whose reason and intention and motives in life are beyond something I could relate to or find some sympathy with, that sort of thing. You know, sociopaths or hate-filled misanthropes in their private lives. If that makes sense,' she added.

He nodded.

'Such thoughts influence all they do,' she continued.

Isaac nodded again. 'It's all perspective, I guess.'

'Not really,' said Lil. 'Some things are just wrong.'

Isaac smiled. 'You're a tough audience,' he said. 'You should open your mind a little more.'

Lil laughed. 'My mind is open enough to allow people who don't agree with me time to see the light and restore themselves. In fact I feel sorry for people who don't agree with me. Because they are wrong. I'm always right – it bores me at this stage.' She said archly and then laughed out loud.

He smiled too. Too much? She wondered.

She was joking, sort of. I'm not a complete idiot she thought. I do listen. Was it getting awkward? She decided to move the conversation on.

'Show me,' she said moving toward him. She could feel the heat off his neck. She longed to stretch her arm around him. He clicked onto an album and handed her his phone. As she had suspected they were pretty, and varying in type and style, from traditional portrait form to surreal. 'They're beautiful,' she said. 'You see, I'm always right.' She chose some favourites and explained her choice as they had entertained and moved her.

He thanked her and she handed his phone back. 'Let me show you my favourite.' He was flicking through lots of pictures. He handed her the phone back, she looked down.

'Oh, ceramic,' she said.

'On oil,' he finished. 'I've stopped doing them, too heavy and my agent doesn't think they are so sellable.'

Lil turned suddenly. 'Your agent?' she said shocked.

'Yes, Phil,' he beamed. 'You'll meet him.'

'You have an agent?' She was astonished and felt completely left behind.

'You have to have one. You've got to be proactive – people don't just come up to you and ask you to sell them some art.'

Lil agreed wholeheartedly. Inside her stomach was lurching, she was a sickening failure even in that. To distract herself and to change her thoughts she looked again.

'It looks like mosaic,' she said.

'It is mosaic,' he said. 'I loved doing them – getting bits and fragments all jumbled together and then if you step back you see the bigger picture. All the damage and the cracks, the broken pieces, the crumbs and chips. They all fit together to make for a perfect whole. I think. All the flaws, all the gaps, the grey areas, the missing bits, the shining parts, the sparkly parts, the dull parts, the shadow and the shade and the light, they all, when arranged and reflected upon, should present harmony and beauty and balance, I hope. Something to be proud of, and sometime that is never the same each time you look at it. If you focus on the small details you lose sight of the sum of the parts. That's how I hope my life will be when I look back on it. I want it to be harmonious and balanced and a lovely mosaic to behold some day, and be something I can be proud of. So all the parts and fragments and the missing pieces should make up someone I can be proud of and a life I could be proud of.'

He looked into the distance.

'You should be proud,' said Lil. 'That is so nice and you are so wonderful. I am so grateful that you like to travel and that I met you.'

Isaac laughed out loud and returned to her. 'You need to travel more,' he said again.

'Why? You travelled and met me. I don't want to travel and meet me. I annoy me enough already without finding myself abroad – it would be too cruel of fate, and a waste of an airline ticket, well, the money.' She laughed.

'What about *your* work?' he asked. 'I would love to

see some.'

Lil reddened a little, uncomfortable. 'It's in storage at the moment,' she said commending herself on the swift use of the word storage, which was a fantastic term to describe boxes under her bed. 'I'd be happy to paint something for you, a gift.'

Isaac laughed. 'You can't do that.'

'Yes, I can. I promise, and I always keep my word. You don't need to worry, you are under no obligation to like it.'

He smiled. 'I'm sure it'd be beautiful,' he said.

'Don't be too sure,' she said.

'But,' he said 'I've always believed that art is an extension of who the artist is and I'm never wrong,' he teased.

She squirmed but laughed.

'I bet your work is beautiful,' he stated again. 'You're beautiful. In fact, I'd love to paint you.'

Lil's head felt dizzy. 'Yes, I liked your surreal work,' she said.

'Portrait,' he said.

She blushed. Her heart pounded. She looked at him, then away. Oh, to have an idea of what to do next!

Silence a while.

Suddenly he sprang up. 'I've got to go,' he said. 'I had no idea of the time, Phil is waiting, we really need to finish my set up for Friday, I am so so sorry Lil.'

Lil stood up, the air was charged with haste. 'Friday?' she said.

He took a crumpled flyer from his pocket and handed it to her. 'It's an exhibition I'm featured in, we want to sell.'

She looked down at the flyer.

'Will you come?' he asked looking as if he was going

to run away at any second. 'I would love if you did – it would mean a lot.'

She nodded.

'I'm so sorry,' he said again. 'I really have to go.'

Lil said it was fine.

He took off swiftly towards the park exit, turned around and shouted, 'I'm going to paint you!' He blew her a kiss then turned and began to almost run.

Lil looked at the flyer and then sat back down and lit a cigarette. Her mind was silent – she had no idea or any thoughts on how the afternoon had gone either way.

Twelve

The next day Lil was still playing and replaying the meeting in her mind. It had ended so abruptly, she thought. Was she expecting too much? He had said he wanted to paint her, so he must think she was attractive, and he had laughed at all the terrible jokes, and even teased her a little.

She didn't know.

He seemed so distant and then when he looked at her, it was like as if there was no one else in the world, he was just focusing on her and seeming to delight in what she was saying. He was, she decided, very transparent. She wasn't sure, but then who was in the early stages such as this? Maybe it was awkward for him too? Perhaps he hadn't much experience either? Maybe it was hard for men too? Maybe she wasn't giving him the right vibes? What are the right vibes? Should I start flirting? But I'm not sure even how. I know some people communicate by flirting with everyone – I don't know how they do it or why – but should I up my game? How do men think in these situations?

She thought of Keith. Perfect. She could consult.

Poor Isaac, she thought suddenly, he is probably unsure too. She felt a surge of warmth and compassion for him. He had said it would mean a lot to him if she went on Friday, and he did shout across a group of people in a park that he wished to paint her. Why her? She could hear them say, *she's no oil painting!* No, that's true.

129

But her portrait is.

She smiled, thinking of him, and rejoiced. He was the bubbles in champagne and the wonder in wonderful. And so delicately awkward, of course he was. Goslings and ducklings and all little -lings came into her mind. She hugged herself in delight. She let her mind wander. She felt heart-swollen, almost drunk, on her new-found lyrical limerence. She found herself wondering if they had met in a previous life, such was their strength of connection, like nothing she had ever known. What had been their relationship? He must feel it too – it would be impossible not to.

The universe had conspired to bring about their reunion. The world had indeed come to her, and what a world, what new kingdoms to discover. She felt almost moved to tears in gratitude.

Later on she sat outside with Keith. He looked at the flyer again. She smoked. And both reflected on the situation.

'He is definitely cute,' agreed Keith.

She smiled. 'Yes. But not too cute, you know, not enough for people to think accusing thoughts of his having low self-esteem or something, you know.'

Keith looked like he plainly didn't know.

'Well, they could, think you know, well, I'm not exactly a supermodel now, am I, more like a three-door-model Ford, on a fat day.'

Keith shook his head in mock despair. 'How old is he?' he asked.

'Why?' asked Lil. 'Does he look very young? He doesn't look too young? I mean, younger than me? I don't look much older than him, do I?' There was a fret in her voice.

Keith shook his head. 'Of course not,' he said loyally.

'I'd say you would both look great together – I was just thinking I looked so old in comparison,' he added.

Lil almost burst with delight. Dear Keith always knew the ways of life and said the right thing. He was so simple and honest. And, having been in a relationship for an age, spoke female like a native. If there was a Nobel Prize for speech he should get it. Forget English, he should give classes to foreigners on how to think the right way and say the right thing. Foreigners being men – that mysterious and charming bunch of aliens who perhaps needed, or at least would benefit from, instruction. Who doesn't benefit from instruction? Who meaning men. He was so grounded and at ease. She envied him that. I should go to the classes too, she thought, how to be grounded and at ease in any situation. Giving birth – grounded and at ease; talking to people – grounded and at ease; getting married – grounded and at ease; getting divorced – grounded and at ease; getting old – grounded and at ease; death – grounded.

She clicked back into the conversation.

Keith handed her back the flyer. 'He's a handsome fellow,' he conceded graciously.

Lil smiled. 'His teeth are perfect. I spent forty minutes on mine last night, with baking soda and coconut oil. All I manged to do really was shred my gums. They looked blood red for around three hours after.'

'So,' asked Keith. 'Did you? Did he?' He shifted in his seat.

Lil shook her head. 'We met in a park,' she said. 'Of course not.'

Keith let out a sigh. 'Did he kiss you?' he asked. 'I'm not asking if he jumped on you.'

She shook her head silently. 'Is that bad? But he did have to leave really suddenly,' she stated in his, or her, defence. She scanned Keith's face.

Keith thought a moment. 'It's not written in stone, and if he had to leave abruptly, it probably interrupted his plan and if he had stayed, things may have developed in a way he would have preferred.'

Lil took this on. This made perfect sense to her. She felt guilty almost for even having the impurity of mind to question Isaac now.

'He,' continued Keith, 'is probably berating himself for not trying. He's probably thinking he was a fool to rush away without trying. He's probably miserable thinking he missed his chance.'

Lil took this piece of intelligence on board. This was news to her. 'Do you think so?' she asked. 'He hasn't messaged me,' she added.

'He's probably embarrassed, and wants to wait and see you in person,' he confirmed.

This thought had not occurred to her at all. She checked her mind for the loopholes or flaws. She couldn't find any. 'So this thing on Friday, should be the third date? Do you think?'

Keith nodded. 'Absolutely.'

She thought again, and then flushed. 'Third date,' she said. 'Do you think he might, you know, expect something? Should I be prepared?'

He looked at her. 'Is that what you want?' he asked softly.

She thought a moment. 'Well, obviously, but I'm not too sure, I hadn't expected this so soon,' she said. 'God.'

Keith laughed. 'Maybe wait for him to kiss you first,' he said, 'and you'll know what's right.'

Lil nodded, more to herself. Suddenly things were complicated.

She looked at the flyer again and at Isaac's photo. She smiled. She thought of her body – it wasn't so bad – years of not ever going out on beaches or in the sun had had its advantages. Her bod had its imperfections, but nothing that would make a man swallow his vomit on sight or throw it up all over her. It was quite a nice body, actually. It didn't have too many miles on it. And the motor still worked, even if the battery had run down a little.

She smiled at Keith as he lit another cigarette. 'You've been in a relationship for – twelve years now?' she asked.

He nodded.

'That's such a long time, well done,' she said. 'That's my idea of success, twelve years. Congratulations. You're a good man.'

He exhaled. 'Why, thank you,' he said.

She was silent again for a moment. 'What's it like?' she asked, 'to have sex with the same person for twelve years? Doesn't it get old? Are you still attracted to her? Is she still sexy for you, or is it duty served? I can't imagine at all.'

She looked enquiringly at him.

He thought a moment. 'It's great' he said.

Lil looked at him. 'Don't say what you're supposed to say. Are you still attracted to her? Is it still: here comes the weekend, lets party? If you know what I mean.'

'Totally,' he said. 'Better – you know what the other one likes and what to do – it's better and longer lasting, it's great, can't complain at all.'

Lil reflected on this. She looked again at Keith. It was good to know. She apologised. 'I just have no idea. I guess it must be nice,' she said, almost to herself.

He nodded.

She continued. 'And it doesn't matter you know? Lines and – well, I'm hardly beach fit or sculpted from marble – I don't look like I've been found at the bottom of a trawler net – but I'm not exactly, well, if I were to appear in a magazine I'd be grateful for the staples in my stomach.' She smiled.

'Most guys aren't into that either,' he said. 'At least I don't think so, and guys aren't sculpted from marble either.'

She nodded. 'I wouldn't like that anyway. It's hard enough having to compete with women, body wise, much less with a guy and his own body. My long-dead dignity would roll over in its unmarked grave.' She smiled. 'Thanks Keith. I'm so sorry, but I've no one to really talk about these things with, it's so hard to know, people don't tell the truth so much. Thank you.' She hugged him. 'I'm lucky to have you.' She put the flyer away. 'Cigarette?'

Later at the bedsit, Lil reflected on their conversation. She was thrilled and grateful to Keith. So, after twelve years it got even better. She loved the idea of waking up beside someone, pulling back the curtains and letting the sun pour over them as they breakfasted and planned that day. It can't be so hard, she thought. She yearned for a complicity, a confelicitous secret of two, a bask of delight. One for which navigating the world was a joyful adventure.

She lit a cigarette.

How nice, she thought, wouldn't that be?

She gazed out of the window and then decided to open her emails. And, looking down them quickly, her blood froze – Christine had emailed again. Lil clicked in her eyes, hurtled over the lines. So, Christine was coming sooner than Lil had realised. She switched off the computer and closed her eyes.

She doesn't have any power, I have the control, she thought. I've already played in that movie – if she thinks I'm going to star in a sequel she is mistaken.

Lil was shaking now.

She poured a glass of wine, or rather a mug, having finally broken her last tall-stemmed stolen-from-a-bar-anyway wine glass. She paced the room trying to breathe. She sat back down. I promised him a painting, she remembered.

She got down on her knees and hunted under her bed. It had been too long. She dragged out her easel, paints, and a dusty but new canvas. She almost screamed with elation when she discovered the paints hadn't gone off. She set up the easel and put Isaac's flyer on the canvas. Lil had said she was a woman of her word, and she was keeping her word as much to herself as to him. She knew exactly what she would paint. Considering he had been born in and around a full moon, she felt this would be the basis. His was a sunny disposition but a lunar landscape would please him, she knew this. She opened her tubes of paint and the smell perfumed the air. It was like an aphrodisiac to her. She felt overwhelmed, like meeting an old friend after years apart. She stood taking in its fragrance, the familiarity causing her to breathe content.

Thirteen

On Friday, having said goodbye to Keith, Lil walked a little nervously toward the gallery where Isaac was having his exhibition. She felt a little self-conscious, having put on mascara and lipstick. Painting canvas is less stressful than painting your face, she thought. She felt pleased. She'd been worried that she might not be able to paint again, but as soon as she'd started she felt everything come back. She would have it done soon. Which was good because she did so hate having a painting go on too long in the making. She lost interest fast.

A little nervously, she approached the gallery, but then remembered that he had invited her.

The people going in all looked very well dressed. But, she thought, she didn't look so bad either, and could reasonably carry herself. She took a deep breath and walked in, smiling and trying to look casual among the suits. She hoped that one day she too would have an exhibition, rather than being the exhibition.

A waiter was walking around with wine. She took a glass, thanking him. She wandered a little looking for Isaac. She saw him. He was wearing skinny jeans, a skinny tie, skinny shirt, and skinny blazer. Skinny. Well he wasn't fat, she thought. His head was thrown back – he was laughing. Of course.

She decided not to go over to him. She felt she looked fine, but didn't wish to embarrass him with the runner-up trophy. She took another glass off a table and walked around looking at the work on the walls, feeling inner delight in her confidence that hers were as good and could hang proudly there too.

Some day, she thought.

The wine was kicking in, she felt very relaxed and slightly hazy as she wandered around. It's all very civilised, she thought, whiling time away in a gallery, with wine, nice. Everyone looked reasonably nice, she thought to herself. She caught her reflection in the glass of a painting. She still had the huge crease from the eye mask she had worn to bed. She had worn it to reduce the bags under her eyes. It had worked, but now she had a lovely long crease nicely crescented across her brow, directly perpendicular to the mark left by her shower cap and its industrial elastic. It looked like a ploughing competition had been held on her face. She was standing in front of a painting of oxen.

How appropriate.

Who paints oxen these days? Someone incredibly bored or someone who finds inspiration in everything, she thought charitably, but concluded that neither would be husband material.

She picked up another glass and wandered around. Isaac was nowhere to be seen. Obviously he would be busy, busy selling his paintings. She wondered if she should leave, she would thank him for inviting her and wish him success in his evening. She felt very pleased by her adult reaction. No sulking or asking him to answer her initial thoughts. She understood this was important to him and it was his moment and she mustn't make it all about her. Very grown up, she thought, I'm a fast learner.

She took another sip.

Pleased that she had decided upon a non-emotional

action grounded in such a neutral and understanding perspective, she thought this was the kind of action an unbiased relationship councillor would celebrate and wish other clients to see and emulate. Lil looked for a place to put her glass down. As she did so she heard him call her.

She turned around.

'Isaac!' she gushed, too loudly and too happily. Her voice was much louder when it was out loud rather than Nay Booing or telling her what to do in her own head. 'Sorry, I was a bit loud, lost in thought,' she said.

'I'm so glad you made it,' he said.

'I wouldn't have missed it for anything – I love your work – I'm a fan,' she smiled. He smelt good, she thought.

'The auction is about to start. Let's go to the back office, would you mind, I hate being in the room when the auctions happen.'

Lil was thrilled. 'Of course, how exciting, rather like going backstage when a performance is on.'

He nodded and led her out of the room, gesturing hello to almost everyone as they did so, until they finally reached a side corridor and came to a door. 'In here,' he said. They went in. Isaac opened a bottle of wine. 'I kept a few in here,' he said.

'Did you buy the wine?' she asked.

'Of course,' he said. 'It's expected, and it does loosen buyers up a bit.'

She took a glass. 'Very smart,' she said, 'although I imagine they don't need loosening. Your work is wonderful.'

They chinked glasses. Lil's heart tumbled a little, now they were alone, it felt all a flurry like a chick in the nest attempting to fly.

Isaac was distracted. Lil assumed he was anxious. Understandably so. She felt at ease not having to do or say anything. Indeed, she wisely thought, right now would be a very bad time. I am learning fast, she thought, well done me. She drank. Delayed gratification and all that. She sloshed some more wine down. Maybe not. Isaac looked far away. She wondered would it look terrible if she helped herself to the wine. As she was weighing this up in her mind, the door burst open.

A man came in.

'I thought I'd find you in here,' he said to Isaac. Isaac jumped up and hugged him. The man was tall, dark, and handsome. Very tall, very dark, and very handsome. So tall, thought Lil, many would enjoy the climb up, not to mention the slide down. The kind of man who would certainly scramble your eggs on a Sunday morning.

Isaac turned to Lil. 'This is Phil – my agent,' he said.

Lil smiled.

Phil came over and shook her hand, telling her it was nice to meet her. She smiled. Quite a handshake, she thought.

'We've sold five already,' he said triumphantly.

Isaac whooped with pleasure.

Lil beamed. 'Congratulations,' she said. 'Wow.'

Phil looked from one to the other and smiled. 'I had better get back out there, at least one of us should be,' he smiled, repeated his pleasure at meeting Lil and left.

'Fantastic,' she said. 'Congratulations.' She wasn't sure what to do next.

Isaac refilled her glass. He was shaking. This was amazing and good for her too, it boded well for their evening together, it took out any suspense, saved her from having to act as a consoling voice of reason about capricious art buyers.

Feeling calm delight, she sat down again.

'Phil is a very attractive man, goodness me,' she laughed.

Isaac nodded. 'But don't get your hopes up, he's married' he said.

Lil flushed. 'That's not what I meant,' she said a little defensively.

Isaac laughed again. 'His wife certainly punched way out of her league getting him,' he said.

Lil was surprised by the tone. 'I'm sure she's equally beautiful,' she said.

Isaac snorted, obviously disagreeing.

Lil wasn't sure she liked it.

'I don't think she has even a pulse much less a personality. How she escaped the drowning the rest of the litter got is beyond me.'

Lil was suddenly sober. She distinctly disliked this and wracked her brain for something to change the subject to.

'And she hates me' added Isaac.

Lil saw a chance in this. 'I doubt that completely, how could anyone possibly hate you?' she said, hoping to veer him somewhere else, anywhere else.

'She's jealous,' he said sharply. 'I've no idea why. I'm no threat to her. I don't have a vagina.'

Lil was lost by now.

'Her husband just prefers hanging out with me, I'm sure of it, I make him laugh more. She hates that, and I'm sure she hates me.'

Lil shook her head but decided against venturing alternatives to his interpretation. She sipped and looked around the room waiting for the topic to change.

'He's hardly ever going to leave her,' continued Issac. 'She's obviously highly threatened by me, she obviously suspects or believes or feels she even knows. She is canny,

I will give her that. But then most animals are.'

That stung, thought Lil, still feeling as if she had walked in on a conversation which had started without her. She felt she had missed some of the key words and was busily now trying to cobble together what in the hell he could be so ferocious about. Everything had seemed so perfect just a whispering ago. She needed clarification.

'Suspects what?' she asked, genuinely looking for an answer. Isaac was lovely and plainly not a sociopathic psychopath. She doubted he could even lie properly, for goodness sake.

Isaac looked at her. 'Good,' he said. 'So it isn't obvious,' he stated cryptically.

'Obvious?' Lil was not enjoying the puzzle.

'Maybe I wish it was then – it would make things easier, but it wouldn't be fair, and I would hate to do anything that could hurt him or make him unhappy. He's the most perfect person I have ever met.'

Isaac looked away.

For Lil the penny dropped. Clang. She felt as if she had been shot in the stomach. She went rigid. She could feel the reddening on her face begin to tingle. Pins and needles were prickling all over now. She let out her held breath. She could hear her own pulse. She felt unbelievably stupid. Idiot! It was Nay Boo, screaming in her head. Idiot. In lipstick, mascara, all done up to be exposed as the idiot you are. Dressed for the occasion. Tarted up twit, way too old for this. Idiot.

She breathed out slowly.

She hated herself. Of course he had never been interested, of course not. He could see what everyone else saw. She felt almost sick at the idea of his reaction should he know. What would be his critique of her appearance? She felt dizzy. He wouldn't be so awful she thought. But was kindness and not saying anything out of pity any better? She felt numb, but needed to shift gear.

'I'm sure he knows, or has an inkling,' she offered, in a soothing and non-shaking voice. Distance was already making itself known.

Isaac looked forlorn. 'He knows I'm gay, of course, that is obvious to everyone, of course.' He smiled. 'How many straight men would go up randomly to a girl in a gallery and start talking?' he laughed. 'It would completely freak you out, wouldn't it?'

Lil found herself nodding in agreement. 'Yes,' she said. 'Or how many straight men would go into a gallery? I'm sure there's a joke in there somewhere – this guy goes into a gallery – '

She laughed, wishing she could be teleported out of the room and back to the bar with Keith. She felt incredibly old and irrelevant.

'Should I say something?' he asked. 'Surely he would appreciate it? It would be such a lot to unburden?' He looked earnestly at her.

Lil felt herself slip back into that comfortable role of confidante and advice-giver. She almost went into autopilot mode, so instantaneous was her resignation. She felt a little guilty about how little she actually cared. It was completely meaningless to her. She checked herself for being so selfish. This was a person like any other in distress. Mentally she gathered herself, best face forward. She reassumed the role effortlessly, like putting back on well-worn comfortable clothes.

Florals.

She sighed, taking in Isaac's troubled face which seemed completely consumed by this one thing.

'You could say something,' she said quietly, 'but what would it achieve? You should probably think about it as it could make everything awkward between you two. He might become alarmed a little, and over-interpret things, and you could run the risk of losing him for ever. He does have a wife. I'm sure she doesn't hate you. And he'd probably tell her. It could all get very messy. I'm sorry for being so honest, but I guess that's what I think.'

She looked for his reaction. He looked miserable now, she thought, feeling a little bad that she had caused a shadow to cross his bloom.

He sniffed. 'I know, you're right. It's so hard, when you love someone, and I know he loves me, and thinks the world of me, but – '

Lil nodded. 'But – ' she repeated.

'Thank you,' he said. 'I'm sure you must know the feeling, you must have fallen in love like this, when you were young, how did you cope?' he looked at her with wide-eyed expectancy.

Lil tried to ignore the cauterization of the bullet hole. She looked away and thought a moment.

'Well,' she began, after looking at his face and feeling a surge of sympathy, as she would for a stranger, or a student of hers, anyone with such an expression of bruised pain. 'I don't really know, I guess I just picked up the pieces, put myself together as best I could and carried on. Sorry, if that's no help,' she said. 'I guess we have to believe things get better. They say a heart isn't a heart until it's been broken a few times, it may be missing the pieces that others carry with them even if they have left our lives, but I don't know,' she said finally. 'I'm not an expert. But you're so young,' she said, pointedly, to place further distance between them, and pre-empt any thoughts or suspicions he might ever have of her ever having considered him; the remaining scraps of her self-respect would hate that. 'You have time – you're so wonderful –

someone will reflect your light at you. I'm sure that someone exists as sure as you exist and are right here in front of me now.' She stood up. 'Come here,' she extended her arms. She hugged him and then kissed his cheek. 'It'll be fine,' she said. She noticed she had left lipstick on his cheek. She took a tissue and cleaned it. Quite the Hollywood moment, she thought. Not the Hollywood ending she had hoped for, but then it often felt to her as if her own life story was in fact just a supporting role in someone else's movie. She sighed. 'Perfect,' she said standing back.

'Thank you,' said Isaac. 'Sorry,' he added.

'There's no need to be sorry,' she stated. 'None at all. Thank you for telling me. I'm happy you could trust me.' She wanted to leave as soon as possible and just get the hell out of there. 'More wine?' she asked him, filling her own.

He nodded. 'I guess we'll be going soon,' he said.

'Going?' said Lil, her heart leaping, glad an ending was in sight.

'Yes, for dinner, to celebrate, you'll have to come too, just Phil and I.'

Lil thanked him, the light of the exit door was blinking at the end of this particular tunnel, but she feigned shock.

'I can't,' she said. 'I thought I was only coming for your exhibition. I have a birthday party to attend, I was going to invite you. You can come after your dinner if you like,' she said.

Isaac looked disappointed. 'I don't know,' he said.

'Well,' said Lil, 'you have my number, just let me know, call me.'

She knew he wouldn't call. Just as well – there was no party. She stretched out her arms. 'I had actually better go.' She hugged him once more. 'Congratulations again,' she said, 'and have a wonderful evening, please don't worry too much.' She smiled and they thanked each other. Lil left and walked back down the corridor to the main door and practically raced outside.

Fourteen

Lil awoke the next morning in a ferociously foul mood. Her night had been unsettling. She had awoken every hour, yet again convinced someone was calling her.

She felt on edge.

Walking to the sink to get some water, she saw that a bottle of wine stood on the countertop. With some left. She poured it, drank, winced. And sat. And looked at her painting. And decided to darken the wood. Not due to her mood – if the painting were to reflect her mood she'd need to kick a hole in it.

She wondered if he would want it now. Or if she would give it to him, rather.

If he wants it he can ask for it, she thought before deciding that was not fair. But she thought a future relationship would probably see her just be his encourager and supporter and she didn't have the energy. She was struck and suddenly questioned herself.

What if she was seen as that?

As a person needing the kindwill of others to keep her standing and walking. She would rather die than be thought of as that. The person in need of others to keep them afloat, That Woman Who – That Person Who – maybe even That Friend Who –

Doesn't every group have one? Was she that one? Her mood worsened at the thought.

Death would be preferable.

146

She felt so furious and would have loved to scream. But furious at who? It was hardly Isaac's fault. He was not responsible for the stupidity of her thoughts or the ridiculous way her mind worked. She wanted to scream with frustration. Anyway, she thought, if I did scream I'd probably have new lines around my mouth, stretchmarks from giving voice to stupid ideas and stupid feelings.

She poured the last of the wine and looked at the canvas. Well, she decided, I did promise him. I suppose if we weren't to meet again it would be a revelation of character proving my motives were not genuine. A new friend is nice, she argued, isn't it?

She looked outside, it was raining.

This was the kind of afternoon that people usually said they loved because it meant staying inside, being warm, eating, doing nice things. It is also the weekend, she thought. She decided to get dressed, get out, get a bottle of wine, and then come back to the painting. Appraising it, she felt it was potentially good but missing something. She wasn't sure what, but that would probably come.

If he can do it, she thought, so can I.

She pootled around before putting on her coat. Wine and some food. Cake. She cheered. Cake was the answer. Not the exact answer but she decided to ignore the question.

On Monday morning Lil sat outside smoking with Keith.

'Goddamnit!' he said, laughing, as she did too. 'Sorry for laughing,'

'Don't be,' she said. 'I do attract them, don't I?'

'Gay?'

'Gay,' she repeated.

'So, that's that?'

'Yes, it would appear so,' said Lil. 'I probably should

have known. People do tend to kiss on a first date, don't they?'

Keith nodded. 'Probably. Seal the deal.'

She nodded. 'He did say that it was obvious, that I should have known. I didn't though – am I blind? It never occurred to me. I have no idea what gay looks like. What does gay look like?' she asked looking at Keith.

Keith exhaled. 'My uncle Rupert.'

'What?' she asked.

'My uncle Rupert' he repeated, 'or Gay Uncle Rupert as we call him.'

Lil was intrigued. 'Rupert?' she said in disbelief. 'I know your grandmother is old, but I had no idea she stretched back to eighteenth-century landed gentry – that's quite the name – Rupert.'

Keith laughed. 'Well,' he explained, 'it was supposed to be Robert, but the clerk filling in the birth certificate didn't understand my grannie's accent. She said Rhubard so Rupert it was and is – Old Gay Uncle Rupert. Not that he would ever admit the old bit. And it's only Gay Uncle Rupert to me and my cousins. He's The Eligible Bachelor to the rest of the family.'

Lil sighed. 'Poor gay uncle Rupert,' she said.

'He argues he never got married because women only wanted his money,' continued Keith. 'Women do love a post office savings account,' he said.

Lil agreed. 'I know I do,' she confirmed. 'A man with a post office savings account, well, I'm overwhelmed.'

They laughed.

'Poor gay uncle Rupert,' repeated Lil.

'He's fine,' said Keith. 'He has his hobbies and his clubs, and takes very good care of himself. His skin is so shiny you can see your own face in it.'

Lil considered this and decided she never wished to

meet gay uncle Rupert. She didn't quite fancy seeing her own blemished, lined face reflected back at her from the flawless complexion of a man two hundred years older than her.

'And for all of that,' she said, 'he still can't get a man either. Five hundred years old and still waiting for the cavalry to come in and meet the dragoon of his dreams. I know the feeling,' she said. 'Poor gay uncle Rupert. I don't want a knight in shining armour, I want a night of shining amour.'

She looked at Keith. 'You have my permission to groan – that was poor,' she said.

He smiled.

'Anyway,' she continued, 'who wouldn't want me?'

'Your mother,' he answered.

She conceded. 'Also my current class. And men. Straight men. Yes, aside from my own mother, my current class, and all the heterosexual men on the planet, who wouldn't want me?'

'I think you forgot to put lesbians on the list,' said Keith.

'Thank you for your help' she laughed. Then sighed. 'Bloody men,' she said. 'Not you Keith, but honestly, the more I think about men the more I consider the genetic similarity between them and dogs. Just throw a ball at a group of either and they will be distracted for hours. You could be in the middle of telling a man that his mother had been thunderballed in a freak meteor incident, and that her ashes had been accidentally swept up and dumped in the council tip, but then watch, should a ball roll by, every single atom and cell in his body concentrate fiercely in order to prevent him from yielding to his instinct to kick it and run around after it, whooping and lolling and almost barking with enthusiasm. Men are so stupid.'

'But you love us,' concluded Keith.

'Well, yes.'

They laughed.

She looked into the distance.

'I suppose I shall just have to get back out there,' she said. 'There are plenty more dogs in the pound, and all that. I'll have to find a stray straight. I don't know what they look like either, though,' she said. She took a cigarette.

'Keith!' she said suddenly. 'If I die alone, you'll be there won't you?'

Keith promised. They laughed.

'I have no idea why I am laughing,' she said.

The Buddha came by. 'Laughing,' he said, 'it's nice to laugh, laughing is good.'

Both stopped.

'You weren't at the meeting,' he said to Lil. 'I thought you were sick, you're normally so professional and considerate, you'd never leave everyone else to sit through a meeting because you didn't feel like it. But everyone's allowed, everyone's special, you're an individual, you're special, it's allowed if you don't want to go to a meeting that everyone else has to go to, you've earned that right,' he stopped talking but was still looking at her.

She was not in the mood. 'Please continue,' she said, 'but let me get a pen and paper to write down the musings and let me sit at your lotus-blossomed feet, oh sagacious one.'

The Buddha looked at Keith.

'Someone is very aggressive today. Be peaceful,' he then bleated at Lil. 'Be a lover, not a fighter. We all have anger, anger is good, but maybe you should have yours checked. I'm just saying,' he nodded at Keith then maundered off.

Keith laughed. 'What a psycho,' he said.

'It's my fault,' said Lil. 'I engaged. I'm a fighter,' she said, and then went on with faux faultlessness. 'My weaponry of choice happens to be love, and comeliness, and fair play with a sense of right and wrong,' she laughed. 'You'll probably find bits of me in sandwich bags in bins all over the city, and my head as a doorstop holding up an umbrella in his flat next week.' She shuddered and laughed. 'Did I miss anything at the meeting anyway?'

Keith shrugged. 'The usual. Well, now, we are only allowed four teaspoons of coffee a day, and fifty millilitres of milk. The budget is tight. And if we want sugar we need to ask at reception. And Being Alive has sponsored the planting of a tree in a sustainable forest. The certificate is on the noticeboard above the photocopier. That's about it,' he said.

Lil smiled. 'Glad I didn't go,' she said.

Keith remembered something. 'There is that staff training day next week. Participation is mandatory.'

Lil groaned. 'Being Alive/Dead Inside. Are we getting paid for it?'

'Chicken Curry said he would look into it,' said Keith.

'So, that's a no,' said Lil. She looked away. 'I need to go shopping,' she said, 'so Christine doesn't think I'm breadline.' She sighed. 'I'll need to gather my arsenal for that,' she said. She looked at Keith.

'It's this week? I forgot. I can still come with you,' he said. 'I'd be very happy to do so.'

Lil was already shaking her head. 'But thank you beloved Keith. I couldn't subject you – but you'll be on standby?' she almost entreated.

'Of course, I have the keys to my car, remember, we found them.'

She smiled weakly, feeling faintly sick at the upcoming visitation. 'I can do this,' she said.

'Of course you can, you have my support all the way,' he confirmed.

Lil looked at him suddenly, taking in his kind, open face, and wasn't sure of what to think. She hugged him. 'I do appreciate you, even if it feels like I'm a self-absorbed cow. I don't mean to be so pathetic,' she said.

'What?' he laughed confused. 'You're definitely not a cow.'

She thanked him. 'I don't have a double D anyway,' she said.

Keith looked bewildered. 'Smoke,' he said offering her one.

She took it. 'I can call you if I need to?' she repeated anxiously.

Keith calmly nodded.

She apologised and they smoked in peaceful silence.

Lil's mind flipped backwards and forwards with anxiety not resting on any one key worry instead just whirling and spinning from one thing to another setting off further spinning and circling . She put her head down and felt exhausted. She tried to tell herself it would come and it would go and soon it would be over. She wished for the tumult to stop a second, but she had to go shopping and she doubted it would let up for that duration.

She smiled at Keith. Students started coming out again. It was time to go.

Fifteen

Lil sat nervously looking at the door to the café. She sat resenting the new clothes she had had to buy. Even cheap clothes were expensive. She looked at the other customers around her. Everyone seemed happy, having a nice time, all pretty normal. Interacting as people do. Even the staff seemed happy. Everyone was enviable, getting on with things in an easy way. She so wanted to be part of that.

She looked at the door expectantly again, beginning to feel extremely noticeable.

Anger began to mount.

Christine was late. Of course she was. It wasn't disrespect, thought Lil, that was too easy a word thrown about willy-nilly. It was just a lack of respect. It's only, 'Lil? She can wait.' Lil was beginning to feel – actually, was it anger? Certainly it was something. She wasn't totally sure. Was it fear? Or was her body on a subconscious level singing a cellular song at being reunited with its progenitor? Was this anxiety, or love even? Was it just painful because it was wrenching itself up and would reassert itself eventually? She didn't know.

She had a headache and was beginning to feel she was being held there against her will.

It was bizarre and it was against her will. She had agreed out of politeness, a sense of doing the right thing. It was not what she had wanted, this meeting with Christine. She hadn't thought of what she had wanted. She knew she wanted to leave right now. It was far too late in the day and too late in her life to pick up some mother-daughter routine and behave as though this was how it had always been or, worse, how it always would be. That was not the past and would not be the future. Lil felt sick. The past and the present were becoming entwined and forming a knot in her stomach and mind. The eddying whorl was making her head pulse. She felt furious.

Christine was thirty minutes late now.

Thirty.

She would probably try to latch on to the end. No chance, thought Lil grimly. She thanked the waiter as he placed another coffee, and wished she had brought a newspaper, it would at least stop her staring at the door. A further ten minutes passed. She wondered if she should leave. She was, however, morbidly curious, and switched off her phone. She had no desire for Christine to know she was in the modern world with a phone that could be called at any time.

She put it in her bag and exhaled. She was shaking a little. Was it rage or nerves? She took another sip. She looked up. Christine was heading toward her.

Lil gulped.

She stood and they embraced.

'Thank you for coming,' began Christine. 'I'm sorry I'm so late, but the hotel I'm staying in put me in a room with a shower only. I bathe. It took them almost an hour to change us.'

Lil, shuddering, felt for the staff, knowing too well the impact a complainer can have, and she could only imagine the steely displeasure and uncompromising attitude Christine would have emitted.

'The staff were very unhelpful, very uneducated,

practically no English, I don't know how these people get jobs.' She took off her coat. She was wearing a very elegant blue dress.

Lil sighed. 'You're hardly in a position to judge. Aren't you an immigrant too?'

'I speak the language!' snapped Christine. 'And I have manners and an education.' She sat back. 'I also had a job lined up, I was a worker. These people may have jobs, but they don't work,' she asserted. 'I worked.' She looked at Lil. 'And he was rude. I hate rudeness. There's no need.' She put her bag on her lap.

'If you spoke *to* them as you're speaking *about* them I'm surprised they're letting you stay there,' said Lil. 'Sounds like they have their work cut out for them, and it's hard enough already.'

Christine was examining her face in a hand mirror. 'I worked. All through my pregnancies I worked. Every single hour in that place, when I was pregnant with you, I worked – don't forget that.'

Lil was silenced. The Institution for the Gentle Care of Mothers and Babies had yet to be spoken of.

Lil looked into her cup, almost empty.

Christine was patting her hair and rearranging her scarf. 'Tom will join us later for supper,' she said. 'He's just fixing the hotel situation. He booked it, he can book it again, right this time.'

Lil exhaled. Tom, Christine's ex-husband, had seemed to her to be a nice man, but she hardly knew him. He had cheated on Christine years ago and was paying for it now, emotionally no doubt, and certainly monthly in cheque form.

Silence fell, the waiter came over. Christine turned away from him. Lil ordered two coffees, hoping by being extra effusive he wouldn't have noticed the snub. He walked away.

Christine, turning back, looked at Lil. 'I must say,' she said, 'I'm very disappointed in you.'

Lil reeled as though she had been slapped. . 'Excuse me?' she said.

Christine failed to recognise, or chose to ignore, the tone. 'I'm disappointed in you. I asked you to email me every day, and you didn't, and you still haven't a passport. I'm disappointed.'

Lil's face was aflame. 'You have no right to say that! How dare you say that to me!'

Christine was unmoved. 'All I'm saying is that I asked you to do this simple thing and you didn't. It doesn't take much time. I can't keep running over here all the time, and I am getting older.' She looked at Lil.

Who was raging inside.

'I have no need to explain myself to you,' she rapped out with full blood-rush to her head now. 'And who in the hell do you think you are to talk to me like that?'

'I am your mother,' said Christine. 'That is who I am, and I'm simply stating the truth,' she said.

Lil was fit to erupt. 'No, you're not,' she accused. 'No, you are not. You are simply a woman who was mother to a child whom she gave up many years ago – that is who you are.' She was shaking.

'I *am* your mother,' repeated Christine, also beginning to get angry. 'If I'm not, who is then?' she said almost sarcastically.

'Necessity,' spat out Lil. 'You were obviously no mother to me, and nor was that insane cruel dragon you let them feed me to almost forty years ago, so it's a little late in the day.'

She couldn't think of how to continue.

Christine looked around them. 'I wasn't responsible

for your placing. I said I was sorry they'd treated you so badly. I didn't know. How could I?'

Lil felt every nerve in her body.

'It was interesting being brought up by people who had such loathing they couldn't even look at me most days. That was interesting when you look back at it, at least. And now you expect me to …'

She stopped, trying to control herself, trying to breathe. She wasn't pleased at being able to go from zero to volcanic in less than a minute.

Lil was silent.

Christine was looking about. And then started at Lil. 'Why don't you let me love you?' she asked angrily. 'Why? I've done everything. I've visited you, three times now, and you've met my children. It's your turn to reciprocate.' She looked vexed.

Lil gasped. 'I don't need to do anything,' she said. 'You looked for me, remember, not I you. And, as I've told you, I have compassion and complete understanding for the young girl who was pregnant. The young you. I never took it personally. I understand you gave up a baby, not me. That is completely fine. Even after you told me you could have kept me, but you were having too much of a good time. I respect that,' said Lil.

Christine turned thunderous. 'I never said that!' she almost shrieked.

'So,' asserted Lil 'I invented that, did I? And what possible reason would I have to invent your saying that?'

Christine was furious now. 'I never said that. I was working. I've told you. I was working, a scarlet whore, with a scarlet letter. I had no choice. I had no choice.' She actually banged her fists on the table.

Lil's head was pounding. 'That is not what you told

me,' she said calmly.

'You can fantasise all you like, but if you fictionalise my past I take exception.'

Lil drank some more coffee.

'I just wanted the truth, that is all, I never judged you or blamed you. In fact, I celebrated your being ahead of your time. And I know you weren't to know about those people, it's probably not even their fault, if you can't stand someone you can't really force it, can you? Even if it is supposed to be your child? I guess some can despise their children, especially when it isn't even theirs. I just wanted the truth, but I can see you are incapable.'

Christine swallowed hard. 'Incapable?' she began. She looked around the room and then back at Lil. 'I am sorry you are so unhappy, really I am,' she said.

Lil's face was pulsating. 'I'm not unhappy,' she said. 'I have a beautiful life.'

'Then why are you so ungrateful?' demanded Christine, 'Especially to someone to whom you are most indebted?'

'I did thank you,' said Lil. 'Don't you remember? I do. It's hard to forget a conversation thanking the woman who gave birth to you for not aborting you. But, thank you, again.' She looked away.

Christine looked at her. 'A little gratitude is not too much to ask for, particularly if there is to be a more intimate mother-child relationship.'

Lil looked at the ceiling.

Intimacy, she thought. Talking to Keith about sex, that was intimate, built over years of trust and friendship, that was intimate. 'I have no idea what you mean by intimate,' she said. 'I'm very happy to meet you when you decide to visit, but if you think our relationship is ever going to evolve beyond what is currently extant, you're mistaken.

I'm so sorry if what you want now differs from what you wanted then, but this is my life, and what I want for my life supersedes what *you* want for my life. You have a life, and a family back home, why don't you focus on them?'

Christine was trying hard to maintain composure. She looked furiously at Lil.

'You're so ungrateful. I have introduced you to my family and opened our lives to you to love you and you turn your back on it. You're so angry. You should learn to forgive. I've forgiven. I forgave those who have trespassed against me, I am liberated and not in bondage to hate and resentment. I chose forgiveness and you're choosing bitterness and anger. I've chosen to let things go.'

Lil was burning. 'Well, yes, I can see, when I look at you I see the picture of zen and love. Please tell me more! Allow me to be like you, so I can one day achieve such a tranquil view on the world.'

She exhaled.

Christine was beginning to shake. 'You'll be sorry one day,' she said.

'Is that a threat, a fear, or a hope?' answered Lil.

Christine readjusted her scarf. 'I can see this is getting me nowhere. I don't know why you're so difficult,' she said.

'Difficult?' practically shrieked Lil. 'Isn't that what those people termed me, always difficult, a difficult child with genetically inherited disorders. I was more amazed by their knowing such vocabulary than insulted by their intended approximation of my bad character.'

Christine was putting on her coat. 'This is not dignified,' she stated, 'and it's beneath me to squabble. I don't need to be here for this.'

'Enjoy the rest of your vacation,' said Lil. 'I hope the bath is perfect.'

Christine looked down on her and then turned and walked away.

Lil watched her go.

Well, that went well, she thought, and almost laughed.

She put her head in her hands and wondered if she should have another coffee. Her head was pounding. She could hardly remember anything that had been said, or rather screamed.

She decided she needed a drink. She beckoned the waiter. 'Sorry for the show,' she said to him.

He shook his head. 'Are you alright?' he asked.

She felt a rush of warmth and appreciation. 'Fine,' she said, and she paid him, gave a tip, said thank you again and walked toward a different exit, for fear of meeting Christine should she decide to come back, obviously she wouldn't, but in case.

Walking out into the sun, she began strolling along, looking at everyone, everyone so serene and peaceful, seemingly, going about their daily business looking calm and normal.

She bought a bottle of wine and went back to the bedsit.

Once in she sat down, let out a huge sigh, and questioned herself. Had she been unfair? Was she wrong? Surely even Christine was better than nothing. The day's heat and noise flashed in front of her, her past searing its way into her mind. How could she ever move on if she was being constantly reconnected with it? After taking a mouthful of the wine, she set the bottle down. And shook her head.

Again, it sounded as if someone was calling her.

Lil, looking around, the sound seemed almost recognisable but just was that tiny bit too unfamiliar to truly tell, ran her hand through her hair. And shook her head again. The voice had gone. She took a deep breath. She looked at her canvas and decided to pick up where she had left off.

Sixteen

Sarah hugged Lil again. 'I'm so sorry,' she said.

'Don't be,' said Lil. 'I'm just happy you were around, it's amazing,' she smiled.

'I wish you'd told me you were meeting her.'

Lil sipped her wine. 'I didn't want to bother you. You're busy, and I could handle it. Sort of.'

Sarah sat back down again and took back up her glass. 'The audacity of her, really.'

Lil nodded. 'She is tenacious, if nothing else,' she said.

'Nice word for her,' said Sarah, 'but are you alright, really?'

Lil shrugged.

'Fine,' she said. 'It was all meaningless anyway, a long charade, very loud, very noisy, and very overheated. All for what? For nothing, at least to me. These last four years have been consumed and wasted since she exploded out of the blue into my life. It's given me nothing. I've achieved nothing. All it did was decentre me and undo any sort of work I may have done in banishing the ghosts of the past. I just want to move on. All she wants is to blame everyone and anyone. Believe it or not I have no blame. I know you think I'm so defensive, and I do have reasons, but I'm not that bad, I think, no, I know.' She sighed. 'Anyway, Keith sends his love.'

Sarah, smiling, moved to change the subject. 'How's

work lately?'

Lil shrugged again.

'The students look upon me as some sort of ancient village elder, like something from science-fiction or a prehistoric movie, it's the greying hair. I'm too old for this. I think the students see me as one step up from a hologram, one dimensional, you know, and that I just switch myself off when class is over. I guess they're not too far from the truth.' She laughed. 'It can get a little lonely,' she added. She looked away.

'You really should get some other work,' said Sarah.

'Of course I should,' agreed Lil a little peeved and tetchy. 'But where? And what? Who wants this now, when they can choose a twenty-four-year-old, fresh-faced, eager, not to mention quick-to-learn and easier-to-manage.'

Sarah sighed. 'You have so much experience, outside the class too. Your organizational skills, your administration, there is so much there.'

Lil shook her head. 'I don't think they see that, and I've no desire to go for an interview and find someone I went to school with, or something, smirking across the table at me. Can you imagine? Dear god.' She shook a little. 'The risk's too great.'

She looked at the ceiling. She was uncomfortable.

That Friend Who –

'Really Lil, please would you consider going to therapy? It helped me so much. Everyone's doing it now, half the country is on antidepressants, there is no shame these days. It may be a little expensive, but you'd save so much, you mightn't need to, well, drink so much.'

Lil's face stung. 'Just in the evenings after work,' she said.

'Yes, but you have a bottle not a glass,' said Sarah.

'I'm not judging. I would probably be the same if it wasn't for the kids.'

Lil felt shame. 'I'm grateful to my wine. If I didn't have some in the evenings I'd probably be completely crazy by now. What the hell else should I do in the evening? Join a book club? Pick up a language class, for god's sake?' She put her head in her hands.

'I could help you find a good one,' said Sarah softly.

Lil shook her head. 'I don't trust psychologists. I worked with some in Being Alive, most of them pursued that calling to sort themselves out. Shrinks just open cans of worms and leave the person to deal with the fallout and the after-mess. I don't need that. I don't need anyone to tell me about me. I don't need myself to be revealed to me. No one knows me better than I do. Too well, in fact. Infuriatingly so.'

Sarah sighed. 'I don't doubt you, but perhaps they could offer insight or devices, so if you ever did meet someone from the past, well, you could have resources and strategies to call upon, ways to manage successfully.

Lil sighed. 'I'll think about it, and that's as big a concession as I can give. Could we please change the subject?'

Sarah, smiling, accepted defeat and they chinked glasses.

'Have you done any painting lately?' asked Sarah.

Lil explained she had started, omitting the reason.

Sarah brightened. 'You know, that's something you would be amazing at – art therapy – have you ever thought of that?'

'You need a qualification,' said Lil.

'Get one,' answered Sarah.

'You need money,' said Lil exasperated.

'You would get funded,' stated Sarah.

Lil was beginning to regret their meeting up. Those who can, do, and those who can't, teach art therapy. She simply nodded.

Sarah topped their glasses up. 'Any men at all?' she tentatively said. 'Can I ask?'

'Of course you can ask,' said Lil. 'And of course not.' She had no desire to relay her recent entry into school-girl hysteria. She cringed at the memory. Her stomach heaved in acute embarrassment. 'I just have to accept that some people attract, and others don't. I'm a don't,' she laughed. 'It's not hugely difficult to understand, it's just chemical or something. It's fine.'

'Nonsense,' said Sarah. 'You're far too guarded. Guys are afraid of you, that's all.'

Lil rolled her eyes. 'Thank you for believing that,' she said. 'Anyway, if a guy isn't prepared to invest time to try to get beyond my well-guarded and celebrated defensiveness and boundaries then he isn't the right guy.'

Sarah was shaking her head. 'Honestly Lil, it's not Hollywood. Your demands are too high.'

Lil didn't say anything.

She didn't want to say that she wanted a man extraordinary, like no other. It wasn't Hollywood, no, but truth was stranger than fiction, and could be more beautiful and more incredible too. She wanted it said of her relationship that if you wrote it no one would believe it. She wanted a man who would be so in tune with her that when they slept, there was a chance they would dream the same dream. Women who lived together often had synchronised menstruation so why not mental or spiritual synchronisation too? It couldn't be too unheard of.

She believed such a possibility of such love existed.

Scientists and technical people had discovered things

and created things because they believed in what they couldn't see or what they were told was impossible. The human race had moved and progressed exactly because people believed. She believed. And wouldn't care if onlookers were nauseated by the sight of the sublime state of her union with the man extraordinary. And by their beliefs, a secret of two. And he wouldn't care either, he'd feel the same. She might be an idiot, but he would be too. They could be idiots together. What is the collective noun for idiots? A refuge? A refuge of idiots. Two together. She did believe this. She couldn't not. She couldn't afford to not believe.

She smiled.

'I know it's not Hollywood,' she said. 'I just don't want to settle for some companionable comfort. I don't want a man who talks about Allen keys, who is this Allen and why is the key named after him, and why does every man on the planet perk up when you mention it and can talk at length about its usefulness and necessity in life? I don't understand and I don't want to understand, I want a man with keys to kingdoms, to other worlds and ways of thinking, even keys to me, I don't want an Allen-key-wearing, grass-cutting, football-watching, beer-drinking everyman. I'm not criticizing him, in fact he's great, he's just not for me, and I'm not for him. That's all I want. Not bloody Allen keys.' She laughed.

Sarah also laughed. 'I actually know what an Allen key is now,' she said.

Lil feigned horror. They laughed again.

Sarah topped up their glasses. 'Here's to romance,' she said. They raised their glasses and drank.

'Thank you for being such a great friend,' said Lil.

Sarah shook with denial. 'Hardly.' And glanced at her watch. 'I'm so sorry, but I'd really better go now. The guys are going to be back in about half an hour.'

'Don't be sorry,' said Lil.

They stood up and hugged.

'I'll call next week,' promised Sarah.

Lil, smiling, turned to walk back to the bedsit. As she walked she couldn't help but feel her life had been raked over, and decided it must look like a complete proclaim-it-on-the-streets disaster. She wondered how she'd got to this point.

She was tired.

She got into the bedsit and sat down. She looked over at the painting. She appreciated the silence it seemed to exude, almost as if it were taking the noise in and, through alchemy, making it into pure solemn beautiful silence, soft and dark, eschewing the garish light of day. She decided to work a little more on it. A little more. You're not a complete disaster, she said to it. Standing in front of it and closing her eyes, she got lost in her reveries.

Seventeen

This was going to be a very long day. Lil, nursing her coffee, looked across at Lickspittle who was holding a very beautiful ornate thermal mug. Lil wished she had thought to bring one. His probably has vodka in it, she thought. And wished she had thought of that too. The Bitch was sat flicking his fingernails repeatedly. He looked at her. She smiled at him, he glared. She decided not to risk any of his sandwiches today.

Keith, smelling of nicotine, came in and sat down beside her.

She smiled. 'This is going to be long,' she said.

'Very long,' he agreed.

Chicken Curry swept into the room. He was wearing a suit complete with waistcoat.

Slightly over the top, thought Lil. Overstuffed Chicken Curry.

Who now looked around at the assembled group. 'Is everyone here' he asked.

No one answered. Lil wondered if he was waiting for those who weren't present to speak up and identify themselves. She felt like putting her hand up.

'Excellent,' he said. 'It is my great honour and privilege to introduce to you all, straight from the beating heart of Being Alive central, Rodney.' He announced this with obvious and cringing pride. Lil almost felt sorry for him. He actually believes this, she thought, all of a wonder, all of a sudden.

Rodney walked into the roar of silence and sullen-eyed looks.

Another part of Lil died inside. Rodney looked as if his clothes had been plastic-painted on. His pot belly as it pressed against his shirt caused an eye-watering sheen. Lil, noticing a nipple nudging at the sheer fabric, felt queasy.

'Thank you,' said Rodney in a robotic voice. It sounded like satnav gone bad. The kind of satnav voice that would direct you off a cliff and then laugh electronically as you plummeted down the ravine.

Lil wondered if anyone had actually ever died from boredom.

'Today is a very special day,' robo-spoke Rodney, as he looked around. 'Could anyone tell me why today is a special day?'

Silence. So much silence that Lil felt she did indeed hear a tree falling in a forest.

She envied the tree.

'Today is a special day,' he continued in his computer programme voice, 'a very special day.' He looked around again.

Lil could feel vital organs shutting down. His was the kind of voice that, were he a doctor at your bedside, would make you use all your last remaining bodily strength and energy to lean weakly across and switch yourself off. And, next, use the last grit of your spirit of life to pull out the plug just to make sure.

Oh. She groaned.

'I can tell you why it's special. It's special because Being Alive is closed today.'

The pain was getting intense and they weren't even five minutes in. Lil found herself thinking that Rodney might have been a nice person before he had died. The only clue to his being a reanimated corpse were the unblinking LED screens where his eyes used to be and a big Being Alive logo embossed on his shirt over where his heart had used to be.

'You close at weekends,' chirped up Lickspittle.

Rodney ignored this. 'We're here today to re-evaluate the service we give our customers,' he said. 'By customers who do you think I mean?' he looked around.

Lil looked at her feet. Silence.

'Of course, by customers, I mean our students,' he said.

Lil still looked at her feet. She was wondering how shoe designers go about designing. Is it just like children drawing? Or is it similar to engineering? How could they improve the design?

'We want our customers to have the greatest time of their lives here,' droned on Rodney. 'We want them to be treated like kings and queens while they are with us.' He looked around.

I'm a Vegan put her hand up.

Rodney nodded at her.

'Hello, yes,' she began. Lil didn't look up. 'I'm sorry,' continued I'm a Vegan nervously, 'but as we're a multinational organisation, with people from all over the world and from different backgrounds and traditions, I don't feel comfortable using such binary terms as king and queen. It's funny, because I'm a vegan, and I think we should be more inclusive. I know myself, because I'm a vegan, and I've experienced discrimination and prejudice and I don't think we should use such old fashioned hierarchical and patriarchal terms in today's world.'

Rodney looked at her.

Lil felt she could hear his eyes click and whorl as they scanned her face and computed the contents of what she had said. He nodded. 'We want our clients to be special,' he said.

'Thank you,' said I'm a Vegan.

Not as special as the bloody employees, thought Lil.

Rodney continued. 'We want our special people to have a special time, here in this special school, in this special city, in your special country.' He stopped.

I'm a Vegan was nodding her head enthusiastically. 'We do,' she said. 'By we, I mean all of us – that's not my pronoun – not that it would be bad if it was – and of course, I agree too,' she hastened.

Lil put her head in her hands and then looked over at Trainwreck who appeared to be examining her reflection in the polish on her acrylic nails. The Buddha was rocking back and forth in his chair. Ominous, thought Lil, glad she was several seats away.

Rodney continued.

'How do we know where to improve and further serve our clients?' he asked. 'Where could we look for clues?'

I'm a Vegan put up her hand. 'Feedback and complaints,' she said, in her best-girl-in-the-form voice.

Rodney looked over at her and blinked. 'Thank you,' he said, 'but we don't like the word complaint. It implies something negative.'

I'm a Vegan blushed and looked around.

Lil decided Rodney had lost his calling and should work for some central intelligence unit. If he spoke at people, half the world's crimes would be confessed to and put away in half a day's work.

'Are we getting paid for this?' suddenly shouted the Buddha. 'And I mean, teacher rate, not admin rate. Admin rate wouldn't cover my backseat let alone the cost of living.'

Chicken Curry looked horrified. 'We have a lovely

lunch included,' he said.

'Soggy sandwiches won't pay my rent,' said the Buddha. 'And the landlord wouldn't even give them to his dog.' He eyeballed Chicken Curry.

The Bitch turned around. 'My sandwiches are not soggy,' he snapped, 'and you'll be lucky to get one you ignorant monkey pig.'

Chicken Curry was further devastated by the show in front of his guest.

Lil covered her face. Ignorant Monkey Pig, she thought. She wanted to laugh.

'Hang on,' said the Buddha. 'I don't appreciate your violence.'

The Bitch was flaring. 'Violence?' he said. 'Violence? You don't know the half of it pet.'

Chicken Curry moved to settle the argument. 'Gentlemen,' he said, 'please, gentlemen.'

The Buddha looked away. The Bitch hmphed, and too turned away.

Chicken Curry, looking over at Rodney, nodded.

'Thank you for your contribution,' said Rodney. 'We don't like the word *complaint* we prefer *words spoken*. What do you think I mean when I refer to *words spoken*?' he asked.

Lil was having a competition now with herself to see how long she could hold her breath.

More silence, with a bit of an edge now.

'*Words spoken*,' continued Rodney, 'are gifts.' He nodded in deference to the imagined astonishment greeting this piece of information. 'Gifts, which are Gentle Information Allowing for Further Triumph – gifts,' he repeated looking around. 'Everyone likes gifts. You like gifts, and you, and you,' he said addressing the tops of people's heads. 'We at Being Alive love gifts. We are grateful and appreciative because gifts allow us to grow. We develop and evolve and provide an even better service. Whoever said you cannot improve upon perfection is out of business now.' He took a moment and smiled at the room.

His smile was more sinister than his voice, thought Lil, making him look like a villain delivering terrible news to a trussed-up-on-strings old enemy.

Rodney took some papers. 'I have some gift vouchers here, I would like you all to take one, and fill them in turning words spoken into words written.' He handed them out. 'Please take a while to reflect, and then I shall collect them.'

Lil glanced sideways at Keith. Both wanted to laugh. This was a new pain.

'Do you have a pen, Rod?' shouted Lickspittle.

Rodney's disapproval rippled. 'For sure,' he said. 'Does anyone else require a writing implement?' he looked around the room. Everyone put their hand up.

Chicken Curry bristled with embarrassment. 'Let me get some,' he said retreating from the room.

Rodney seemed to switch off, doubtless gone into standby-energy-saving mode thought Lil.

Chicken Curry came back with a box of pens.

'Thanks sir,' said Lickspittle. 'You're always so helpful. I don't think you get enough recognition or appreciation around here, thanks,' he said.

Rodney switched back on. 'Please don't tarry, but hasten to task,' he said.

'Sorry Rod,' said Lickspittle.

After a short while Rodney collected the *gift vouchers*. 'Thank you,' he stated. 'Let's see what we have here, and then we can discuss in groups and come up with ...' he paused, 'solutions. We can then check our service style with an enactment of the situation and our responsive solution.'

Upon which he took a *gift voucher* and cleared his throat.

'I don't like my teacher,' he read. Nodding, he put it beside him and picked another. 'I'm sexually attracted to my teacher.'

He cleared his throat.

'That's a common one I hear all the time, Rod,' said Lickspittle.

Rodney put it down and took another. 'My host family is three hours away.' He nodded and put it down. 'My host family make me eat murdered animals.' He put it down and took another. 'I feel uncomfortable at the exploitation and substandard treatment of my teacher who is a peaceful educator, corporate.' Rodney didn't continue reading, he put it down. He looked around the room and then at Chicken Curry. 'Shall we have an early lunch, now?' he said.

Within seconds chairs upended as everyone hurtled toward the door. Chicken Curry being closest was first out.

Rodney sat down in front of his laptop.

After lunch and having been hunted down by Chicken Curry, who had rounded people up from bathrooms, the smoking area, the cleaning cupboards, under the stairs, behind single standing whiteboards, behind plastic shrubberies, behind doors, from outside window ledges on the ground floor, and from under the desk at reception, they began.

Rodney stood waiting. 'Thank you for lunch,' he stated.

The Bitch nodded.

Rodney continued. 'Being Alive prides itself on

supreme customer service and we wish to unveil our new strategy to impart our philosophy going forward. Our researchers have spent five years developing this at our labs and central hub of expertise and experience.' He switched on his laptop. The image of a cartoon bee appeared on the wall behind him. 'What's this?' he asked.

Lil felt the torment of the tedium rush back.

'Is it a bee?' asked Ladymine fearfully.

'Thank you,' said Rodney. 'It's a bee.'

I'm a Vegan darted a look at Ladymine. She was put out as she'd also known the answer.

'But it is not just any bee,' continued Rodney. 'It's a busy bee.'

Lil looked at the cartoon. He didn't look that busy. He had a big grin on his face and his arms were raised in a macho look-at-my-muscles pose.

'Because we, at Being Alive, are busy bees.' He let the metaphor sink in a moment. 'We've come up with the five Bs of customer service.' He smiled again.

Lil felt a chill.

Rodney began to expound. 'At Being Alive we like our staff to be, well, alive. We like our staff to be passionate, full of smile and song. A smile,' he said not smiling, 'can change the world. Second, be brave. Bees are brave. They travel far and wide to make their honey. We like our staff to travel the extra mile for our clients,' he said.

Work extra for free, thought Lil.

'Third, be compassionate. Bees work together in a hive. We like our staff to work together for the greater good,' he said.

Money for the owner, thought Lil.

'Four, be decisive. Bees make decisions, sometimes difficult ones, and take responsibility,' he said.

Take the blame then, thought Lil.

'And finally, five, be enthusiastic. Bees work and are busy little bees but they never doubt or question their job. We like our staff to be enthusiastic about their work and remember the importance of giving Being Alive your very best,' he said.

Follow blindly and never object or question anything, thought Lil.

Rodney stood back. 'This is easy for you all,' he said. 'Just be fantastic, bees are fantastic, the world relies on bees, and our clients rely on you. If you're fantastic they'll have a fantastic time and endorse us. Should we do this,' he continued, 'success will be guaranteed.' He clicked on his laptop. Success GuaranBeed popped up in bubble letters beneath the bee.

Lil groaned, but out loud.

Rodney scanned the room to identify the source of discontent.

Lil smiled at him.

He double took.

Was that sweat on his brow? she wondered. Could it lead to malfunctioning?

He turned around to face them.

'I have one last surprise for you,' he announced.

Lil felt as if she couldn't breathe, she needed to get out soon.

Rodney clicked on his laptop. A video popped up. Suddenly disco music started to pound out. A group of senior management flashed up on the screen, wearing bee antennae, bumblebee-stripy-woolly tops, and clip-on wings. They began to sing in unison, 'We are busy little bees, full of honey, busy little bees, bright and sunny, busy little bees, we love our job, busy little bees, going bob, bob, bob.' They broke into a choreographed dance move singing the chorus and adding in buzzing sounds and smiling all the while doing what looked like junior acting class, day two, imitations of bees.

Lil's jaw dropped and she gaped, absolutely horror struck. Make it stop, she thought.

The video ended and Rodney clicked on his laptop. 'Catchy, isn't it? I think you'll agree it's creating quite a buzz,' he said to the dumbfounded room.

Lil was ashen faced and numb from the shock.

'So, now it is your turn,' said Rodney. He produced a bag and proceeded to take out bee antennae, woolly jumpers, headbands, and wings. 'Let's show the world what busy bees you are,' he said. 'I will stand in front to go through the choreography to rehearse before we film,' he said.

Lil felt wildly panicked and sick. She looked at Keith who raised his eyebrows looking fairly aghast too. This cannot be happening, thought Lil, her heart pounding. This cannot be happening! She felt almost out of her body as she watched I'm a Vegan and Ladymine go and check out the bee outfits.

No, she thought, absolutely no.

Lil watched as much barrelling and shoving went on around the bag. She felt dizzy. Suddenly adrenalised, she rushed to Chicken Curry and assailed him with a tumult of symptoms of illness and fled the room. As she rushed out onto the street and dashed in the direction of the bedsit she was pulsing with rage. This was where she worked, this was what she, to all external viewers, had dedicated her life to. This, no one would believe it, had to be experienced to be believed, as a place in general. But now this.

She felt soiled, degraded, and taken for an absolute fool.

Just how stupid and unthinking did they think she

was? Obviously very stupid and very unthinking. She felt gaspingly sick, she was shaking. This was beyond anything, this was what she was doing, this was her life, how had she come to this, how did this happen? Racing along, thinking of Sarah and Holly and all the others with their lives, she wanted to scream. Rage lifted her step as she sped.

Even Christine had made a success of herself.

They all had.

Lil was blind with fury. There's no one to blame, she thought, there's no one except yourself. How did you do this to yourself? Why did you do this to yourself? She was speeding now. She got to the bedsit and slammed the door behind her.

There was a letter on the floor.

She ripped it open.

Notice from the landlord informing her of her final date to vacate. Lil wanted to scream or slam her head against the wall. Anything to distract her from the now. How on earth has my life come to this? She seemed to be screaming at herself inside. How did you do this to yourself?

She was shaking.

Looking at her canvas, she wished for a moment to crawl inside it, to be embraced by its silence and haven. What's the goddamn point it's only a bloody painting anyway, she said. What does that even matter? You're an idiot, you idiot! She shook her head. She remembered her idea of the refuge of idiots, just when she couldn't hate herself more. You're an idiot, she said, the idiot, the ultimate idiot. Of course no one would want you, you're a goddamned idiot. Oh, thank god I didn't mention that theory out loud, for once, she said. What is the point? I hate this, I hate it so much. She sank down onto her bed and put her head on her knees and, against her will and wish, she began to cry.

I don't understand, she thought. I just don't understand.

Eighteen

Several hours later Lil woke up. She was still fully clothed and very dehydrated. It was dark outside. She had no idea of the time. Shaking her head, she heard it again, that voice. She switched on her lamp. The light did not dispel the mood, nor silence the voice that she was sure she could still hear. She looked out of the window. She glanced over at her canvas.

She could still hear it.

Deciding she needed air, and disobeying her instinct, she forged forward and walked outside to the backyard of the building. The air was cool against her heated brow. She walked through the gate which led into a small local park. The moon was high. She felt wretched, overly tired, and sure that the voice was getting louder and clearer in the settled peace of the night. As she walked, she saw a fox. It stood and looked at her a few moments before slinking away. The moon clouded over and a breeze rustled the leaves in the trees. It was soothing, so she walked towards the sound.

Then she stopped. Her eyes made out a figure. She adjusted her vision.

It was tall and seemed to beckon.

As if in sleep, she walked toward him. A man. A man standing in the thicket. A tall, beautiful man, with long black hair and a face as pale and perfect as a reflection of the moon above. He stood sombre and still, a vision of dignity and serenity almost from another world. He spoke to her while smiling.

'I knew you would come to me,' he said, 'I've been waiting.'

Lil gasped at his beauty which was beyond anything she had seen, male or female.

'You seem tired tonight,' he said softly. 'The world is being cruel, far too cruel, to you. I knew you'd come. You need rest,' he said. 'Rest from the fear piled upon fear, silence away from these night skies which, if you listen closely, are filled with the scream and pain of torment. A choric lament of the anguish of the unjustly afflicted, the cries of the virtuous and brave, who are destroyed by the vile and the small.'

He looked deeply into her.

'You need a rest,' he went on. 'A rest far from a world where suffering brings joy and the crush of the virtuous is silenced in the fray. You need a rest from the knowledge that, no matter how hard you try, your efforts will remain as effective as a single grain of sand against the tidal flood of prejudice, hate, and torture all inflicted joyfully and knowingly. You can never win against that. You will never ever win. It will continue as it always has. You don't need that, you don't deserve it.'

He looked even more deeply into her.

'Why continue?' he appealed. 'Why? It's yielded you no reward, you're loveless, you're alone. Surely you don't think that will change? Does anything really matter? Does anything really change? You may try, but there'll always be others whose humanity will shame you. Why must you continue to do this to yourself? You have the choice. You have struggled bravely. Come with me. No one loves you as I, no one understands you as I. I can give you love like none you have ever known. I can give you peace and bring you rest.'

He moved towards her, gazing deeply into her eyes.

'Come with me, just kiss me. When was the last time you were kissed? When do you think you will ever be kissed again? Kiss me,' he said softly.

Lil felt overcome and dazzled by his pulchritude. Her heart sounded the night.

She closed her eyes, opening them, she looked deeply at him and felt desperately that she longed to, to touch those soft lips, to be kissed. Overhead a bat flew. Lil stood frozen a moment, looking at him. And then she turned almost without thinking and ran. She ran and ran, back through the park, back through the gate, through the yard, and into the bedsit. In her speed she tripped up and fell knocking into her canvas which crashed to the floor. Without picking it up she got into bed and covered herself with her quilt and soon blacked out.

When she woke up again, several hours later, her head hurt. She was quivering all over, shaking with cold. She felt beyond awful. She went to her canvas and picked it up. Placing it back on the easel she glanced at it. She noticed that on it, where her hand had fallen, there seemed to be a shape in the thicket. On closer inspection she discerned a figure, of a man with long black hair. She sat back down and worried that truly, this time, she was losing her mind.

Nineteen

Keith hugged her, and then hugged her again. 'I've missed you a lot,' he said. 'You look amazing, just incredible.'

Lil smiled at him. 'Two weeks of not being here can do that to a person,' she said.

'Two weeks of not Being Alive,' suggested Keith.

'Something like that,' laughed Lil.

He flicked his cigarette. 'We'd better go inside – there's a meeting'.

Lil flicked hers too. 'Of course there is,' she said.

They walked in.

Chicken Curry was at the top of the room when they walked in. 'Here she is now,' he announced.

Everyone applauded.

Lil went bright pink.

Chicken Curry looked down his long Roman nose and smiled. 'We have gathered here to express our gratitude and deep thanks for all you have done and all you have contributed to Being Alive over the years. All of us cannot express enough of how highly we think of you and we thank you.'

He moved forward and presented her with a large bouquet of flowers.

Lil felt tears spring.

Chicken Curry continued. 'If you should ever change your mind, know that our door is always open for you. As you know the school is going from strength to strength and we would love to welcome you back.'

Everyone applauded again. Chicken Curry awkwardly hugged her.

Lil was a little overcome. 'Thank you everyone,' she stated. 'I will miss you all, thank you, thank you.'

Everyone cheered again. She opened the card which had come with the flowers. Inside were well wishes from everyone, from Ladymine to Trainwreck. She blinked away tears.

Lickspittle came forward. 'I know you like leather, and you like vintage.' He gave her a green leather vintage bag.

'It's beautiful,' she gushed. 'Honestly, you shouldn't have.'

Lickspittle shook his head. She hugged him and then hugged each of the others assembled. She thanked everyone profusely again, and said goodbye. It felt strange, almost as if she were watching herself in a way.

She went back outside for a final cigarette with Keith.

'I'm going to miss you,' he said. 'But it looks like we might be going travelling very soon, before we, well, I'm probably going to go back to finance, we are thinking of maybe starting a family.'

Lil hugged him overjoyed. 'How perfect, the world needs more of your genes,' she gushed. 'Amazing.'

Keith laughed and disagreed about the world's needs.

Suddenly Lil felt engulfed with sadness. 'I shall see you next week,' she said, 'for a beer.'

He nodded enthusiastically.

She smiled. 'Thank you, Keith, for being such a wonderful friend, thank you.'

Keith shook his head in disagreement and smiled. 'Any plans yet?' he asked.

Lil took a deep breath. 'Well, yes,' she said, 'I'm

going to pick up the pieces, put them back together, and reflect on what it adds up to and where to go next, for there is most definitely a next. I wish to become acquainted with this new who I am, whoever that is, and, you know, take control, move on in life.'

Keith looked suitably impressed. 'Sounds like a plan,' he said approvingly.

Lil laughed. 'Yes, probably very long overdue, but better belated than never.'

Also published by Piwaiwaka Press:
www.piwaiwakapress.org

Tatami Burns

Madden Hay

ISBN: 978-1-7385926-3-0

127 x 203mm (5 x 8 in)

Page count: 212

Lynley finds herself unexpectedly alone in Japan after her girlfriend cancels her teaching contract at the last minute. They'll have a long-distance relationship and meet up again in a year to travel together. Or will they? Loneliness and anxiety threaten to overwhelm Lynley. Luckily, another expat's living nearby, a flamboyant, fun-loving, but sometimes obnoxious fag who she can at least hang out with.

A story about young expats discovering and questioning themselves, each other, and the world. A touching, funny story about understanding and challenging the rules of groups, both large and small, of relationships, and of boundaries.

And the Birds Fled to the Bush

Helen Mae Innes

ISBN: 978-1-7385926-7-8

127 x 203mm (5 x 8 in)

Page count: 226

In the ruins of suburbia everyone is just trying to grow and preserve some veggies, catch a fish or deer or two, avoid government officials and their eviction notices, and keep up with the local goss. Meanwhile, Anton, a specialist in birdsong, arrives hoping to conduct research in the surrounding hills. His project is regarded with ire or indifference by all except Tim, a weird loner living in the bush, whose speech is odd and behaviour odder.

An unlikely trio of young men are forced to work together to achieve their individual and collective aims in a post-earthquake world. They battle against and working with nature, the officious community board, and their absurd proclamations, and a community of hardcase characters.

The Unused Life of Tito Lopez

Luis Luna

ISBN: 978-1-7385926-4-7

127 x 203mm (5 x 8 in)

Page count: 300

A clever, hopeful, young graduate, Tito López, is poised at the entry to adulthood as well as a whole new millennium. Living in a provincial Mexican city at the turn of the 21st century he wants what most of us want … a career, love, happiness. But will he find any of them on Cerro del Calvario?

What's up with his nunnish clever sister Angelita? Will the deer's eye work? Who's the mysterious blond god, Salvador? The Unused Life of Tito López portrays the Lopez family in a way that will seem familiar to those from middle-class suburban families almost anywhere else in the world. Meanwhile, readers from outside Mexico will be intrigued by the sense of other, parallel, exotic, existences in our contemporary world.

Not Swinging, Swooning

Stevan Eldred-Grigg

ISBN: 978-1-7385926-6-1

152 x 228mm (6 x 9 in)

Page count: 254

It's early in the morning,' a boy writes in his diary, 'on the first day of the first year of the most modern decade in the whole of human history. Get in the groove!' The boy, Stevan, is seven years old and one of the middle kids in a nuclear family in a twice-mortgaged new bungalow in a new cul-de-sac in a suburb during the Space Age.

Not Swinging, Swooning is a story about a boy's dreams, dreads, hopes, fears and adventures. A story about elbowing and being elbowed by siblings, aunts, uncles, cousins, neighbours, friends, teachers. A story about pop songs the boy thought were groovy, and about yarns spelled by the olds. A story about being a boy, in a suburb, about becoming, or trying to become, a young man in the mod optimistic hi-gloss world of the sixties of last century.